THE BUSIE BODY
SUSANNA CENTLIVRE

D1523516

INTRODUCTION

Susanna Centlivre (1667?-1723) in *The Busie Body*(1709) contributed to the stage one of the most successful comedies of intrigue of the eighteenth and nineteenth centuries. This play, written when there was a decided trend in England toward sentimental drama, shows Mrs. Centlivre a strong supporter of laughing comedy. She had turned for a time to sentimental comedy and with one of her three sentimental plays, *The Gamester* (1704), had achieved a great success. But her true bent seems to have been toward realistic comedies, chiefly of intrigue: of her nineteen plays written from 1700 to 1723, ten are realistic comedies. Three of these proved very popular in her time and enjoyed a long stage history:*The Busie Body* (1709); *The Wonder: A Woman Keeps a Secret* (1714); and *A Bold Stroke for a Wife* (1717).*The Busie Body* best illustrates Mrs. Centlivre's preference for laughing comedy with an improved moral tone. The characters and the plot are amusing but inoffensive, and, compared to those of Restoration drama, satisfy the desire of the growing eighteenth-century middle-class audience for respectability on the stage.

The theory of comedy on which *The Busie Body* rests is a traditional one, but Mrs. Centlivre's simple pronouncements on the virtues of realistic over sentimental comedy are interesting because of the controversy on this subject among critics and writers at this time. In the preface to her first play, *The Perjur'd Husband* (1700), she takes issue with Jeremy Collier on the charge of immorality in realistic plays. The stage, she believes, should present characters as they are; it is unreasonable to expect a "Person, whose inclinations are always forming Projects to the Dishonor of her Husband, should deliver her Commands to her Confident in the Words of a Psalm." In a letter written in 1700 she says: "I think the main design of Comedy is to make us laugh." (Abel Boyer, *Letters of Wit, Politicks, and Morality*, London, 1701, p. 362). But, she adds, since Collier has taught religion to the "Rhiming Trade, the Comick Muse in iiTragick Posture sat" until she discovered Farquhar, whose language is amusing but decorous and whose plots are virtuous. This insistence on decorum and virtue indicates a concession to Collier and to the public. Thus in the preface to *Love's Contrivance*(1703), she reiterates her belief that comedy should amuse but adds that she strove for a "modest stile" which might not "disoblige the nicest ear." This modest style, not practiced in early plays, is achieved admirably in *The Busie Body*. Yet, as she says in the epilogue, she has not followed the critics who balk the pleasure of the audience to refine their taste; her play will with "good humour, pleasure crown the Night." In dialogue, in plot, and particularly in the character of the amusing but inoffensive Marplot, she fulfills her simple theory of comedy designed not for reform but for laughter.

Mrs. Centlivre followed the practices of her contemporaries in borrowing the plot for *The Busie Body*. The three sources for the play are: *The Devil Is an Ass* (1616) by Jonson; *L'Etourdi* (1658) by Molière; and *Sir Martin Mar-all or The Feigned Innocence* (1667) by Dryden. From *The Devil Is an Ass*, Mrs. Centlivre borrowed minor details and two episodes, one of them the amusing dumb scene. This scene, though a close imitation, seems more amusing in *The Busie Body* than in Jonson's play, perhaps because the characters, especially Sir Francis Gripe and Miranda, are more credible and more fully portrayed. From the second source for *The Busie Body*, Molière's *L'Etourdi*, I believe Mrs. Centlivre borrowed the framework for her parallel plots, the theme of Marplot's blundering, and the name and general character of Marplot. But she has improved what she borrowed. She places in Molière's framework more credible women characters than his, especially in the charming Miranda and the crafty Patch; she constructs a more skillful intrigue plot for the stage than his subplot and emphasizes Spanish customs in the lively Charles-Isabinda-Traffick plot. Mrs. Centlivre concentrates on Marplot's blundering, whereas Molière concentrates on the servant Mascarille's schemes. Marplot's funniest blunder, in the "monkey" scene, is entirely original as far as I know (IV, iv). But her greatest change is in the character of Marplot, who in iiiher hands becomes not so much stupid as human and irresistibly ludicrous. Mrs. Centlivre's style is of course inferior to that of Molière. In the preface to *Love's Contrivance* (1703), in speaking of borrowings from Molière, she said that borrowers "must take care to touch the Colors with an English Pencil, and form the Piece according to our Manners." Of course her touching the "Colors with an English Pencil" meant changing the style of Molière to suit the less delicate taste of the middle-class English audience.

A third source for *The Busie Body* is Dryden's *Sir Martin Mar-all* (1667). Since Dryden followed Molière with considerable exactness, it would be difficult to prove beyond doubt that Mrs. Centlivre borrowed from Molière rather than from Dryden. Yet I believe, after a careful analysis of the plays, that she borrowed from Molière. She made of *The Busie Body* a comedy of intrigue based on the theme and plot used by both Molière and Dryden, but she omitted the scandalous Restoration third plot which Dryden had added to Molière. Her characters are English in speech and action, but they lack the coarseness apparent in Dryden's *Sir Martin Mar-all*. Though it is impossible to prove the exact sources of Mrs. Centlivre's borrowings, there is no doubt that she has improved what she borrowed.

Whatever the truth may be about Mrs. Centlivre's use of her sources, her play remained in the repertory of acting plays long after *L'Etourdi* and *Sir Martin Mar-all* had disappeared. *The Busie Body* opened at the Drury Lane Theater on May 12, 1709. Steele, who listed the play in *The Tatler* for May 14, 1709, does not mention the length of the run. Thomas Whincop says that the play ran thirteen nights (*Scanderbeg*, London, 1747, p. 190), but Genest says the play had an opening run of seven nights (*Some Account of the English Stage from the Restoration in 1660 to 1830*, II, 419). The play remained popular throughout the eighteenth and nineteenth centuries. Genest lists it as being presented in twenty-three seasons from 1709 to 1800. It was certainly presented much more frequently than this record shows, for Dougald MacMillan in *The Drury Lane Calendar* lists fifty-three ivperformances from 1747-1776, whereas Genest records two performances in this period. The greatest number of performances in any season was fourteen in 1758-59, the year David Garrick appeared in the play. From the records available *The Busie Body* seems to have reached its greatest popularity in England in the middle and late eighteenth century and the early part of the nineteenth century. William Hazlitt, in the "Prefatory Remarks" to the Oxberry acting edition of 1819, says *The Busie Body* has been acted a "thousand times in town and country, giving delight to the old, the young, and the middle-aged."

The Busie Body enjoyed a similar place of importance in the stage history of America but achieved its greatest popularity, in New York at least, in the nineteenth century. First performed in Williamsburg on September 10, 1736, the play was presented fifteen times in New York in the eighteenth century. In the nineteenth century forty-five performances were given in New York in sixteen seasons from 1803 to 1885 (George Odell, *Annals of the New York Stage*). *The Busie Body* is frequently cited with *The Rivals* and *The School for Scandal* for opening seasons and for long runs by great actors.

The text here reproduced is from a copy of the first edition now in the library of the University of Michigan.

Jess Byrd
Salem College

THE
BUSIE BODY:
A
COMEDY.
As it is Acted at the
THEATRE-ROYAL
IN
DRURY-LANE,
By Her Majesty's Servants.

Written by Mrs. SUSANNA CENTLIVRE.

Quem tulit ad scenam ventoso Gloria curru,
Exanimat lentus Spectator, sedulus inflat.
Sic Leve, sic parvum est, animum quod laudis avarum
Subruit aut reficit—
Horat. Epist. Lib. II. Ep. 1.

L O N D O N ,
Printed for BERNARD LINTOTT, at the *Cross-Keys*
between the Two *Temple-Gates* in *Fleet-street.*

TO THE
RIGHT HONOURABLE
JOHN Lord *SOMMERS,*
Lord-President of Her HAJESTY'<u>s</u> most
Honourable Privy-Council.

May it please Your Lordship,
    AS it's an Establish'd Custom in these latter Ages, for all Writers, particularly the Poetical, to shelter their Productions under the Protection of the most Distinguish'd, whose Approbation

produces a kind of Inspiration, much superior to that which the *Heathenish* Poets pretended to derive from their Fictitious *Apollo*: So it was my Ambition to Address one of my weak Performances to Your Lordship, who, by Universal Consent, are justly allow'd to be the best Judge of all kinds of Writing.

I was indeed at first deterr'd from my Design, by a Thought that it might be accounted unpardonable Rudeness to obtrude a Trifle of this Nature to a Person, whose sublime Wisdom moderates that Council, which at this Critical Juncture, over-rules the Fate of all *Europe*. But then I was encourag'd by Reflecting, that *Lelius* and *Scipio*, the two greatest Men in their Time, among the *Romans*, both for Political and Military Virtues, in the height of their important Affairs, thought the Perusal and Improving of *Terence*'s Comedies the noblest way of Unbinding their Minds. I own I were guilty of the highest Vanity, should I presume to put my Composures in Parallel with those of that Celebrated *Dramatist*. But then again, I hope that Your Lordship's native Goodness and Generosity, in Condescension to the Taste of the Best and Fairest part of the Town, who have been pleas'd to be diverted by the following SCENES, will excuse and overlook such Faults as your nicer Judgment might discern.

And here, my Lord, the Occasion seems fair for me to engage in a Panegyrick upon those Natural and Acquired Abilities, which so brightly Adorn your Person: But I shall resist that Temptation, being conscious of the Inequality of a Female Pen to so Masculine an Attempt; and having no other Ambition, than to Subscribe my self,

My Lord,

Your Lordship's

Most Humble and

Most Obedient
Servant,

SUSANNA
CENTLIVRE.

PROLOGUE.
By the Author of TUNBRIDGE-WALKS.

THO' *modern Prophets were expos'd of late,*
The Author cou'd not Prophesie his Fate;
If with such Scenes an Audience had been Fir'd,
The Poet must have really been Inspir'd.
But these, alas! are Melancholy Days
For Modern Prophets, and for Modern Plays.
Yet since Prophetick Lyes please Fools o'Fashion,
And Women are so fond of Agitation;
To Men of Sense, I'll Prophesie anew,
And tell you wond'rous things, that will prove true:
Undaunted Collonels will to Camps repair,
Assur'd, there'll be no Skirmishes this Year;
On our own Terms will flow the wish'd-for Peace,
All Wars, except 'twixt Man and Wife, will cease.
The Grand Monarch may wish his Son a Throne,
But hardly will advance to lose his own.
This Season most things bear a smiling Face;
But Play'rs in Summer have a dismal Case,
Since your Appearance only is our Act of Grace.
Court Ladies will to Country Seats be gone,
My Lord can't all the Year live Great in Town,
Where wanting Opera's, Basset, *and a Play,*
They'll Sigh and stitch a Gown, to pass the time away.
Gay City-Wives at Tunbridge *will appear,*
Whose Husbands long have laboured for an Heir;
Where many a Courtier may their Wants relieve,
But by the Waters only they Conceive.
The Fleet-street *Sempstress—Toast of* Temple *Sparks,*
That runs Spruce Neckcloths for Attorney's Clerks;

At Cupid*'s* Gardens *will her Hours regale,*
Sing fair Dorinda, *and drink Bottl'd Ale.*
At all Assemblies, Rakes are up and down,
And Gamesters, where they think they are not known.
  Shou'd I denounce our Author's fate to Day,
To cry down Prophecies, you'd damn the Play:
Yet Whims like these have sometimes made you Laugh;
'Tis Tattling all, like Isaac Bickerstaff.
  Since War, and Places claim the Bards that write,
Be kind, and bear a Woman's Treat to-Night;
Let your Indulgence all her Fears allay,
And none but Woman-Haters damn this Play.

EPILOGUE.

  IN me you see one Busie-Body *more;*
Tho' you may have enough of one before.
With Epilogues, the Busie-Body*'s Way,*
We strive to help; but sometimes mar a Play.
At this mad Sessions, half condemn'd e'er try'd,
Some, in three Days, have been turn'd off, and dy'd,
In spight of Parties, their Attempts are vain,
For like false Prophets, they ne'er rise again.
Too late, when cast, your Favour one beseeches,
And Epilogues prove Execution Speeches.
Yet sure I spy no Busie-Bodies *here;*
And one may pass, since they do ev'ry where.
Sowr Criticks, Time and Breath, and Censures waste,
And baulk your Pleasure to refine your Taste.
One busie Don ill-tim'd high Tenets Preaches,
Another yearly shows himself in Speeches.
Some snivling Cits, wou'd have a Peace for spight,
To starve those Warriours who so bravely fight.
Still of a Foe upon his Knees affraid;
Whose well-hang'd Troops want Money, Heart, and Bread.
Old Beaux, who none not ev'n themselves can please,
Are busie still; for nothing——but to teize
The Young, so busie to engage a Heart,
The Mischief done, are busie most to part.
Ungrateful Wretches, who still cross ones Will,
When they more kindly might be busie still!
One to a Husband, who ne'er dreamt of Horns,
Shows how dear Spouse, with Friend his Brows adorns.
Th' Officious Tell-tale Fool, (he shou'd repent it.)
Parts three kind Souls that liv'd at Peace contented,
Some with Law Quirks set Houses by the Ears;
With Physick one what he wou'd heal impairs.
Like that dark Mob'd up Fry, that neighb'ring Curse,
Who to remove Love's Pain, bestow a worse.
Since then this meddling Tribe infest the Age,
Bear one a while, expos'd upon the Stage.
Let none but Busie-Bodies *vent their Spight!*
And with good Humour, Pleasure crown the Night!

Dramatis Personæ.
MEN.

Sir *George Airy.* A Gentleman of Four Thousand a Year in Love with *Miranda*	Acted by Mr. *Wilks.*
Sir *Francis Gripe.* Guardian to *Miranda* and *Marplot*, Father to *Charles*, in Love with *Miranda.*	Mr. *Estcourt.*

Charles. Friend to *Sir George*, in Love with *Isabinda*.   Mr. *Mills.*

  Sir *Jealous Traffick.* A Merchant that had liv'd sometime in *Spain*, a   Mr. *Bulloc*
great Admirer of the *Spanish* Customs, Father to *Isabinda*.   *k.*

  Marplot. A sort of a silly Fellow, Cowardly, but very Inquisitive to   Mr. *Pack.*
know every Body's Business, generally spoils all he undertakes, yet without
Design.

  Whisper. Servant to *Charles.*   Mr. *Bulloc*
                                            *k*jun.

WOMEN.

  Miranda. An Heiress, worth Thirty Thousand Pound, really in Love   Mrs. *Cross*
with Sir *George*, but pretends to be so with her Guardian Sir *Francis*.   .

  Isabinda. Daughter to Sir *Jealous*, in Love with *Charles*, but design'd for   Mrs. *Roger*
a *Spanish* Merchant by her Father, and kept up from the sight of all Men.   *s.*

  Patch. Her Woman.   Mrs. *Saund*
                                            ers.

  Scentwell. Woman to *Miranda.*   Mrs. *Mills*
                                            .

  1B

THE
BUSIE BODY.
A C T I. S C E N E *T h e P a r k .*
Sir George Airy *meeting* Charles.

Cha.
HA! Sir *George Airy!* A Birding thus early, what forbidden Game rouz'd you so soon? For no
lawful Occasion cou'd invite a Person of your Figure abroad at such unfashionable Hours.
  Sir *Geo.* There are some Men, *Charles*, whom Fortune has left free from Inquietudes, who
are diligently Studious to find out Ways and Means to make themselves uneasie.
  Cha. Is it possible that any thing in Nature can ruffle the Temper of a Man, whom the four
Seasons of the Year compliment with as many Thousand Pounds, nay! and a Father at Rest with
his Ancestors.
  Sir *Geo.* Why there 'tis now! a Man that wants Money thinks none can be unhappy that has
it; but my Affairs are in such a whimsical Posture, that it will require a Calculation of my Nativity
to find if my Gold will relieve me or not.
  Cha. Ha, ha, ha, never consult the Stars about that; Gold has a Power beyond them; Gold
unlocks the Midnight Councils; Gold out-does the Wind, becalms the Ship, or fills her Sails; Gold
is omnipotent below; it makes whole Armies fight, or fly; It buys even Souls, and bribes the
Wretches to 2betray their Country: Then what can thy Business be, that Gold won't serve thee
in?
  Sir *Geo.* Why, I'm in Love.
  Cha. In Love— Ha, ha, ha, ha; In Love, Ha, ha, ha, with what, prithee, a *Cherubin!*
  Sir *Geo.* No, with a Woman.
  Cha. A Woman, Good, Ha, ha, ha, and Gold not help thee?
  Sir *Geo.* But suppose I'm in Love with two—
  Cha. Ay, if thou'rt in Love with two hundred, Gold will fetch 'em, I warrant thee, Boy. But
who are they? who are they? come.
  Sir *Geo.* One is a Lady, whose Face I never saw, but Witty as an Angel; the other Beautiful
as *Venus*—

5

Cha. And a Fool—

Sir Geo. For ought I know, for I never spoke to her, but you can inform me; I am charm'd by the Wit of One, and dye for the Beauty of the Other?

Cha. And pray, which are you in Quest of now?

Sir Geo. I prefer the Sensual Pleasure, I'm for her I've seen, who is thy Father's Ward *Miranda.*

Cha. Nay then, I pity you; for the Jew my Father will no more part with her, and 30000 Pound, than he wou'd with a Guinea to keep me from starving.

Sir Geo. Now you see Gold can't do every thing, *Charles.*

Cha. Yes, for 'tis her Gold that bars my Father's Gate against you.

Sir Geo. Why, if he is this avaricious Wretch, how cam'st thou by such a Liberal Education?

Cha. Not a Souse out of his Pocket, I assure you; I had an Uncle who defray'd that Charge, but for some litte Wildnesses of Youth, tho' he made me his Heir, left Dad my Guardian till I came to Years of Discretion, which I presume the old Gentleman will never think I am; and now he has got the Estate into his Clutches, it does me no more good, than if it lay in *Prester John*'s Dominions.

Sir Geo. What can'st thou find no Stratagem to redeem it?

3B2*Cha.* I have made many Essays to no purpose; tho' Want, the Mistress of Invention, still tempts me on, yet still the old Fox is too cunning for me— I am upon my last Project, which if it fails, then for my last Refuge, a Brown Musquet.

Sir Geo. What is't, can I assist thee?

Cha. Not yet, when you can, I have Confidence enough in you to ask it.

Sir Geo. I am always ready, but what do's he intend to do with *Miranda?* Is she to be sold in private? or will he put her up by way of Auction, at who bids most? If so, Egad, I'm for him: my Gold, as you say, shall be subservient to my Pleasure.

Cha. To deal ingeniously with you, Sir *George*, I know very little of Her, or Home; for since my Uncle's Death, and my Return from Travel, I have never been well with my Father; he thinks my Expences too great, and I his Allowance too little; he never sees me, but he quarrels; and to avoid that, I shun his House as much as possible. The Report is, he intends to marry her himself.

Sir Geo. Can she consent to it?

Cha. Yes faith, so they say; but I tell you, I am wholly ignorant of the matter. *Miranda* and I are like two violent Members of a contrary Party, I can scarce allow her Beauty, tho' all the World do's; nor she me Civility, for that Contempt, I fancy she plays the Mother-in-law already, and sets the old Gentleman on to do mischief.

Sir Geo. Then I've your free Consent to get her.

Cha. Ay and my helping-hand, if occasion be.

Sir Geo. Pugh, yonder's a Fool coming this way, let's avoid him.

Cha. What *Marplot*, no no, he's my Instrument; there's a thousand Conveniences in him, he'll lend me his Money when he has any, run of my Errands and be proud on't; in short, he'll Pimp for me, Lye for me, Drink for me, do any thing but Fight for me, and that I trust to my own Arm for.

Sir Geo. Nay then he's to be endur'd; I never knew his Qualifications before.

4

Enter Marplot *with a Patch cross his Face.*

Marpl. Dear *Charles*, your's,— Ha! Sir *George Airy*, the Man in the World, I have an Ambition to be known to *(aside.)* Give me thy Hand, dear Boy—

Cha. A good Assurance! But heark ye, how came your Beautiful Countenance clouded in the wrong place?

Marpl. I must confess 'tis a little *Mal-a-propos*, but no matter for that; a Word with you, *Charles*; Prithee, introduce me to Sir *George*— he is a Man of Wit, and I'd give ten Guinea's to—

Cha. When you have 'em, you mean.

Marpl. Ay, when I have 'em; pugh, pox, you cut the Thread of my Discourse— I wou'd give ten Guinea's, I say, to be rank'd in his Acquaintance: Well, 'tis a vast Addition to a Man's Fortune, according to the Rout of the World, to be seen in the Company of Leading Men; for then we are all thought to be Politicians, or Whigs, or Jacks, or High-Flyers, or Low-Flyers, or Levellers—and so forth; for you must know, we all herd in Parties now.

Cha. Then a Fool for Diversion is out of Fashion, I find.

Marpl. Yes, without it be a mimicking Fool, and they are Darlings every where; but prithee introduce me.

6

Cha. Well, on Condition you'll give us a true Account how you came by that Mourning Nose, I will.

Marpl. I'll do it.

Cha. Sir *George*, here's a Gentleman has a passionate Desire to kiss your Hand.

Sir Geo. Oh, I honour Men of the Sword, and I presume this Gentleman is lately come from *Spain* or *Portugal*—by his Scars.

Marpl. No really, Sir *George*, mine sprung from civil Fury, happening last Night into the Groom-Porters—I had a strong Inclination to go ten Guineas with a sort of a, sort of a—kind of a Milk Sop, as I thought: A Pox of the Dice he flung out, and my Pockets being empty as *Charles* 5knows they sometimes are, he prov'd a surly *North-Britain*, and broke my Face for my Deficiency.

Sir Geo. Ha! ha! and did not you draw?

Marpl. Draw, Sir, why, I did but lay my Hand upon my Sword to make a swift Retreat, and he roar'd out. Now the Deel a Ma sol, Sir, gin ye touch yer Steel, Ise whip mine through yer Wem.

Sir Geo. Ha, ha, ha,

Cha. Ha, ha, ha, ha, fase was the Word, so you walk'd off, I suppose.

Marp. Yes, for I avoid fighting, purely to be serviceable to my Friends you know—

Sir Geo. Your Friends are much oblig'd to you, Sir, I hope you'll rank me in that Number.

Marpl. Sir *George*, a Bow from the side Box, or to be seen in your Chariot, binds me ever yours.

Sir Geo. Trifles, you may command 'em when you please.

Cha. Provided he may command you—

Marpl. Me! why I live for no other purpose— Sir *George*, I have the Honour to be carest by most of the reigning Toasts of the Town, I'll tell 'em you are the finest Gentleman—

Sir Geo. No, no, prithee let me alone to tell the Ladies—my Parts—can you convey a Letter upon Occasion, or deliver a Message with an Air of Business, Ha!

Marpl. With the Assurance of a Page and the Gravity of a Statesman.

Sir Geo. You know *Miranda!*

Marpl. What, my Sister *Ward?* Why, her Guardian is mine, we are Fellow Sufferers: Ah! he is a covetous, cheating, sanctify'd Curmudgeon; that Sir *Francis Gripe* is a damn'd old—

Char. I suppose, Friend, you forget that he is my Father—

Marpl. I ask your Pardon, *Charles*, but it is for your sake I hate him. Well, I say, the World is mistaken in him, his Out-side Piety, makes him every Man's Executor, and his Inside Cunning, makes him every Heir's Jaylor. Egad, *Charles*, I'm half persuaded that thou'rt some *Ward* too, and never of 6his getting: For thou art as honest a Debauchee as ever Cuckolded Man of Quality.

Sir Geo. A pleasant Fellow.

Cha. The Dog is Diverting sometimes, or there wou'd be no enduring his Impertinence: He is pressing to be employ'd and willing to execute, but some ill Fate generally attends all he undertakes, and he oftner spoils an Intreague than helps it—

Marpl. If I miscarry 'tis none of my Fault, I follow my Instructions.

Cha. Yes, witness the Merchant's Wife.

Marpl. Pish, Pox, that was an Accident.

Sir Geo. What was it, prithee?

Ch. Why, you must know, I had lent a certain Merchant my hunting Horses, and was to have met his Wife in his Absence: Sending him along with my Groom to make the Complement, and to deliver a Letter to the Lady at the same time; what does he do, but gives the Husband the Letter, and offers her the Horses.

Marpl. I remember you was even with me, for you deny'd the Letter to be yours, and swore I had a design upon her, which my Bones paid for.

Cha. Come, Sir *George*, let's walk round, if you are not ingag'd, for I have sent my Man upon a little earnest Business, and have order'd him to bring me the Answer into the Park.

Marpl. Business, and I not know it, Egad I'll watch him.

Sir Geo. I must beg your Pardon, *Charles*, I am to meet your Father here.

Ch. My Father!

Sir Geo. Aye! and about the oddest Bargain perhaps you ever heard off; but I'll not impart till I know the Success.

Marpl. What can his Business be with Sir *Francis?* Now wou'd I give all the World to know it; why the Devil should not one know every Man's Concern.

(Aside.

Cha. Prosperity to't whate'er it be, I have private Affairs too; over a Bottle we'll compare Notes.

7

7*Marpl. Charles* knows I love a Glass as well as any Man, I'll make one; shall it be to Night? Ad I long to know their Secrets.

(Aside.

Enter Whisper.

Whis. Sir, Sir, Mis *Patch* says, *Isabinda*'s Spanish Father has quite spoil'd the Plot, and she can't meet you in the Park, but he infallibly will go out this Afternoon, she says; but I must step again to know the Hour.

Marpl. What did *Whisper* say now? I shall go stark Mad, if I'm not let into this Secret.

(Aside.

Cha. Curst Misfortune, come along with me, my Heart feels Pleasure at her Name. Sir *George*, yours; we'll meet at the old place the usual Hour.

Sir Geo. Agreed; I think I see Sir *Francis* yonder.

(Exit.

Cha. Marplot, you must excuse me, I am engag'd.

(Exit.

Marpl. Engag'd, Egad I'll engage my Life, I'll know what your Engagement is.

(Exit.

Miran. (Coming out of a Chair.) Let the Chair wait: My Servant, That dog'd Sir *George* said he was in the Park.

Enter Patch.

Ha! Mis *Patch* alone, did not you tell me you had contriv'd a way to bring *Isabinda* to the Park?

Patch. Oh, Madam, your Ladiship can't imagine what a wretched Disappointment we have met with: Just as I had fetch'd a Suit of my Cloaths for a Disguise: comes my old Master into his Closet, which is right against her Chamber Door; this struck us into a terrible Fright— At length I put on a Grave Face, and ask'd him if he was at leisure for his Chocolate, in hopes to draw him out of his Hole; but he snap'd my Nose off, No, I shall be busie here this two Hours; at which my poor Mistress seeing no way of Escape, order'd me to wait on your Ladiship with the sad Relation.

Miran. Unhappy *Isabinda!* Was ever any thing so unaccountable as the Humour of Sir *Jealousie Traffick.*

8*Patch.* Oh, Madam, it's his living so long in *Spain*, he vows he'll spend half his Estate, but he'll be a Parliament-Man, on purpose to bring in a Bill for Women to wear Veils, and the other odious *Spanish* Customs— He swears it is the height of Impudence to have a Woman seen Barefac'd even at Church, and scarce believes there's a true begotten Child in the City.

Miran. Ha, ha, ha, how the old Fool torments himself! Suppose he could introduce his rigid Rules—does he think we cou'd not match them in Contrivance? No, no; Let the Tyrant Man make what Laws he will, if there's a Woman under the Government, I warrant she finds a way to break 'em: Is his Mind set upon the *Spaniard* for his Son-in-law still?

Patch. Ay, and he expects him by the next Fleet, which drives his Daughter to Melancholy and Despair: But, Madam, I find you retain the same gay, cheerful Spirit you had, when I waited on your Ladiship.— My Lady is mighty good-humour'd too, and I have found a way to make Sir *Jealousie* believe I am wholly in his Interest, when my real Design is to serve her; he makes me her Jaylor, and I set her at Liberty.

Miran. I know thy Prolifick Brain wou'd be of singular Service to her, or I had not parted with thee to her Father.

Patch. But, Madam, the Report is that you are going to marry your Guardian.

Miran. It is necessary such a Report shou'd be, *Patch.*

Patch. But is it true, Madam?

Miran. That's not absolutely necessary.

Patch. I thought it was only the old Strain, coaxing him still for your own, and railing at all the young Fellows about Town; in my Mind now, you are as ill plagu'd with your Guardian, Madam, as my Lady is with her Father.

Miran. No, I have Liberty, Wench, that she wants; what would she give now to be in this *dissabilee* in the—open Air, nay more, in pursuit of the young Fellow she likes; for that's my Case, I assure thee.

Patch. As for that, Madam, she's even with you; for tho' 9**C**she can't come abroad, we have a way to bring him home in spight of old *Argus.*

Miran. Now *Patch*, your Opinion of my Choice, for here he comes— Ha! my Guardian with him; what can be the meaning of this? I'm sure Sir *Francis* can't know me in this Dress— Let's observe 'em.

(They withdraw.

8

Sir Fran. Verily, Sir *George,* thou wilt repent throwing away thy Money so, for I tell thee sincerely, *Miranda,* my Charge do's not love a young Fellow, they are all vicious, and seldom make good Husbands; in sober Sadness she cannot abide 'em.

Miran. (Peeping.) In sober Sadness you are mistaken—what can this mean?

Sir Geo. Look ye, Sir *Francis,* whether she can or cannot abide young Fellows is not the Business; will you take the fifty Guineas?

Sir Fran. In good truth— I will not, for I knew thy Father, he was a hearty wary Man, and I cannot consent that his Son should squander away what he sav'd, to no purpose.

Mirand. (Peeping.) Now, in the Name of Wonder, what Bargain can he be driving about me for fifty Guineas?

Patch. I wish it ben't for the first Night's Lodging, Madam.

Sir Geo. Well, Sir *Francis,* since you are so conscientious for my Father's sake, then permit me the Favour, *Gratis.*

Miran. (Peeping.) The Favour! Oh my Life! I believe 'tis as you said, *Patch.*

Sir Fran. No verily, if thou dost not buy thy Experience, thou wou'd never be wise; therefore give me a Hundred and try Fortune.

Sir Geo. The Scruples arose, I find, from the scanty Sum— Let me see—a Hundred Guineas— *(Takes 'em out of a Purse and chinks 'em.)* Ha! they have a very pretty Sound, and a very pleasing Look— But then, *Miranda*— But if she should be cruel—

Miran. (Peeping.) As Ten to One I shall—

10Sir *Fran.* Ay, do consider on't, He, he, he, he.

Sir Geo. No, I'll do't.

Patch. Do't, what, whether you will or no, Madam?

Sir Geo. Come to the Point, here's the Gold, sum up the Conditions—

Sir Fran. (Pulling out a Paper.)

Miran. (Peeping.) Ay for Heaven's sake do, for my Expectation is on the Rack.

Sir Fran. Well at your own Peril be it.

Sir Geo. Aye, aye, go on.

Sir Fran. Imprimis, you are to be admitted into my House in order to move your Suit to *Miranda,* for the space of Ten Minutes, without Lett or Molestation, provided I remain in the same Room.

Sir Geo. But out of Ear shot—

Sir Fran. Well, well, I don't desire to hear what you say, Ha, ha, ha, in consideration I am to have that Purse and a hundred Guineas.

Sir Geo. Take it—

(Gives him the Purse.

Miran. (Peeping.) So, 'tis well it's no worse, I'll fit you both—

Sir Geo. And this Agreement is to be perform'd to Day.

Sir Fran. Aye, aye, the sooner the better, poor Fool, how *Miranda*and I shall laugh at him— Well, Sir *George,* Ha, ha, ha, take the last sound of your Guineas, Ha, ha, ha.

(Chinks 'em.)(Exit.

Miran. (Peeping.) Sure he does not know I am *Miranda.*

Sir Geo. A very extraordinary Bargain I have made truly, if she should be really in Love with this old Cuff now— Psha, that's morally impossible—but then what hopes have I to succeed, I never spoke to her—

Miran. (Peeping.) Say you so? Then I am safe.

Sir Geo. What tho' my Tongue never spoke, my Eyes said a thousand Things, and my Hopes flatter'd me hers answer'd 'em. If I'm lucky—if not, 'tis but a hundred Guineas thrown away.

*(*Miranda *and* Patch *come forwards.*

Miran. Upon what Sir *George?*

11C2Sir *Geo.* Ha! my *Incognito*—upon a Woman, Madam.

Miran. They are the worst Things you can deal in, and damage the soonest; your very Breath destroys 'em, and I fear you'll never see your Return, Sir *George,* Ha, ha!

Sir Geo. Were they more brittle than *China,* and drop'd to pieces with a Touch, every Atom of her I have ventur'd at, if she is but Mistress of thy Wit, ballances Ten times the Sum— Prithee let me see thy Face.

Miran. By no means, that may spoil your Opinion of my Sense—

Sir Geo. Rather confirm it, Madam.

Patch. So rob the Lady of your Gallantry, Sir.

9

Sir *Geo.* No Child, a Dish of Chocolate in the Morning never spoils my Dinner; the other Lady, I design a set Meal; so there's no danger—

Miran. Matrimony! Ha, ha, ha; what Crimes have you committed against the God of Love, that he should revenge 'em so severely to stamp Husband upon your Forehead—

Sir *Geo.* For my Folly in having so often met you here, without pursuing the Laws of Nature, and exercising her command— But I resolve e'er we part now, to know who you are, where you live, and what kind of Flesh and Blood your Face is; therefore unmask and don't put me to the trouble of doing it for you.

Miran. My Face is the same Flesh and Blood with my Hand, Sir*George*, which if you'll be so rude to provoke.

Sir *Geo.* You'll apply it to my Cheek— The Ladies Favours are always Welcome; but I must have that Cloud withdrawn. *(Taking hold of her.)* Remember you are in the *Park*, Child, and what a terrible thing would it be to lose this pretty white Hand.

Miran. And how will it sound in a *Chocolate-House*, that Sir*George Airy* rudely pull'd off a Ladies Mask, when he had given her his Honour, that he never would, directly or indirectly endeavour to know her till she gave him Leave.

Patch. I wish we were safe out.

(Aside.

Sir *Geo.* But if that Lady thinks fit to pursue and meet me at every turn like some troubl'd Spirit, shall I be blam'd 12if I inquire into the Reality? I would have nothing dissatisfy'd in a Female Shape.

Miran. What shall I do?

(Pause.

Sir *Geo.* Ay, prithee consider, for thou shalt find me very much at thy Service.

Patch. Suppose, Sir, the Lady shou'd be in Love with you.

Sir *Geo.* Oh! I'll return the Obligation in a Moment.

Patch. And marry her?

Sir *Geo.* Ha, ha, ha, that's not the way to Love her Child.

Miran. If he discovers me, I shall die— Which way shall I escape?— Let me see.

(Pauses.

Sir *Geo.* Well, Madam—

Miran. I have it— Sir *George*, 'tis fit you should allow something; if you'll excuse my Face, and turn your Back (if you look upon me I shall sink, even mask'd as I am) I will confess why I have engag'd you so often, who I am, and where I live?

Sir *Geo.* Well, to show you I'm a Man of Honour I accept the Conditions. Let me but once know those, and the Face won't be long a Secret to me.

(Aside.

Patch. What mean you, Madam?

Miran. To get off.

Sir *Geo.* 'Tis something indecent to turn ones Back upon a Lady; but you command and I obey. *(Turns his Back.)* Come, Madam, begin—

Miran. First then it was my unhappy Lot to see you at *Paris(Draws back a little while and speaks)* at a Ball upon a Birth-Day; your Shape and Air charm'd my Eyes; your Wit and Complaisance my Soul, and from that fatal Night I lov'd you.*(Drawing back.)* And when you left the Place, Grief seiz'd me so— No Rest my Heart, no Sleep my Eyes cou'd know.—

Last I resolv'd a hazardous Point to try,
And quit the Place in search of Liberty.

(Exit.

13Sir *Geo.* Excellent— I hope she's Handsome— Well, Now, Madam, to the other two Things: Your Name, and where you live?— I am a Gentleman, and this Confession will not be lost upon me.— Nay, prithee don't weep, but go on—for I find my Heart melts in thy Behalf— speak quickly or I shall turn about— Not yet.— Poor Lady, she expects I shou'd comfort her; and to do her Justice, she has said enough to encourage me. *(Turns about.)* Ha? gone! The Devil, jilted? Why, what a Tale has she invented—of *Paris*, Balls, and Birth-Days.— Egad I'd give Ten Guineas to know who this Gipsie is.— A Curse of my Folly— I deserve to lose her; what Woman can forgive a Man that turns his Back.

The Bold and Resolute, in Love and War,
To Conquer take the Right, and swiftest way;
The boldest Lover soonest gains the Fair,
As Courage makes the rudest Force obey,
Take no denial, and the Dames adore ye,
Closely pursue them and they fall before ye.

14

ACT the Second.

Enter Sir Francis Gripe, Miranda.

Sir *Fran.*

HA, ha, ha, ha, ha, ha, ha.

Miran. Ha, ha, ha, ha, ha, ha; Oh, I shall die with Laughing.— The most Romantick Adventure: Ha, ha! what does the odious young Fop mean? A Hundred Pieces to talk an Hour with me; Ho, ha.

Sir *Fran.* And I'm to be by too; there's the Jest; Adod, if it had been in Private, I shou'd not have car'd to trust the young Dog.

Mirand. Indeed and Indeed, but you might *Gardy.*— Now methinks there's no Body Handsomer than you; So Neat, so Clean, so Good-Humour'd, and so Loving.—

Sir *Fran.* Pretty Rogue, Pretty Rogue, and so thou shalt find me, if thou do'st prefer thy *Gardy* before these Caperers of the Age, thou shalt see the Queen's Box on an *Opera* Night; thou shalt be the Envy of the Ring (for I will Carry thee to *Hide-Park*) and thy Equipage shall Surpass, the what—d'ye call 'em Ambassadors.

Miran. Nay, I'm sure the Discreet Part of my Sex will Envy me more for the Inside Furniture, when you are in it, than my Outside Equipage.

Sir *Fran.* A Cunning Bagage, a faith thou art, and a wise one too; and to show thee thou hast not chose amiss, I'll this moment Disinherit my Son, and Settle my whole Estate upon thee.

Miran. There's an old Rogue now: *(Aside.)* No, *Gardy,* I would not have your Name be so Black in the World— You know my Father's Will runs, that I am not to possess my Estate, without your Consent, till I'm Five and Twenty; you shall only abate the odd Seven Years, and make me Mistress of my Estate to Day, and I'll make you Master of my Person to Morrow.

15Sir *Fran.* Humph? that may not be safe— No *Chargy,* I'll Settle it upon thee for *Pin-mony;* and that will be every bit as well, thou know'st.

Miran. Unconscionable old Wretch, Bribe me with my own Money— Which way shall I get out of his Hands?

(Aside.

Sir *Fran.* Well, what art thou thinking on, my Girl, ha? How to Banter Sir *George?*

Miran. I must not pretend to Banter: He knows my Tongue too well: *(Aside.)* No, *Gardy,* I have thought of a way will Confound him more than all I cou'd say, if I shou'd talk to him Seven Years.

Sir *Fran.* How's that? Oh! I'm Transported, I'm Ravish'd, I'm Mad—

Miran. It wou'd make you Mad, if you knew All, *(Aside.)* I'll not Answer him one Word, but be Dumb to all he says—

Sir *Fran.* Dumb, good; Ha, ha, ha. Excellent, ha, ha, I think I have you now, Sir *George:* Dumb! he'll go Distracted— Well, she's the wittiest Rogue— Ha, ha, Dumb! I can but Laugh, ha, ha, to think how damn'd Mad he'll be when he finds he has given his Money away for a a Dumb Show. Ha, ha, ha.

Miran. Nay, *Gardy,* if he did but know my Thoughts of him, it wou'd make him ten times Madder: Ha, ha, ha.

Sir *Fran.* Ay, so it wou'd *Chargy,* to hold him in such Derision, to scorn to Answer him, to be Dumb: Ha, ha, ha, ha.

Enter Charles.

Sir *Fran.* How now, Sirrah, Who let you in?

Char. My Necessity, Sir.

Sir *Fran.* Sir, your Necessities are very Impertinent, and ought to have sent before they Entred.

Char. Sir, I knew 'twas a Word wou'd gain Admittance no where.

Sir *Fran.* Then, Sirrah, how durst you Rudely thrust that upon your Father, which no Body else wou'd admit?

16*Char.* Sure the Name of a Son is a sufficient Plea. I ask this Lady's Pardon if I have intruded.

Sir *Fran.* Ay, Ay, ask her Pardon and her Blessing too, if you expect any thing from me.

Miran. I believe yours, Sir *Francis,* in a Purse of Guinea's wou'd be more material. Your Son may have Business with you, I'll retire.

Sir *Fran.* I guess his Business, but I'll dispatch him, I expect the Knight every Minute: You'll be in Readiness.

Miran. Certainly! my Expectation is more upon the wing than yours, old Gentleman.

[Exit.

Sir Fran. Well, Sir!

Char. Nay, it is very Ill, Sir; my Circumstances are, I'm sure.

Sir Fran. And what's that to me, Sir: Your Management shou'd have made them better.

Char. If you please to intrust me with the Management of my Estate, I shall endeavour it, Sir.

Sir Fran. What to set upon a Card, and buy a Lady's Favour at the Price of a Thousand Pieces, to Rig out an Equipage for a Wench, or by your Carelessness enrich your Steward to fine for Sheriff, or put up for Parliament-Man.

Char. I hope I shou'd not spend it this way: However, I ask only for what my Uncle left me; Your's you may dispose of as you please, Sir.

Sir Fran. That I shall, out of your Reach, I assure you, Sir. Adod these young Fellows think old Men get Estates for nothing but them to squander away, in Dicing, Wenching, Drinking, Dressing, and so forth.

Char. I think I was born a Gentleman, Sir; I'm sure my Uncle bred me like one.

Sir Fran. From which you wou'd infer, Sir, that Gaming, Whoring, and the Pox, are Requisits to a Gentleman.

Char. Monstrous! when I wou'd ask him only for a Support, he falls into these unmannerly Reproaches; I must, tho' against my Will, employ Invention, and by Stratagem relieve my self.

(Aside.

17D*Sir Fran.* Sirrah, what is it you mutter, Sirrah, ha? *(Holds up his Cane.)* I say, you sha'n't have a Groat out of my Hands till I Please—and may be I'll never Please, and what's that to you?

Char. Nay, to be Robb'd, or have one's Throat Cut is not much—

Sir Fran. What's that, Sirrah? wou'd ye Rob me, or Cut my Throat, ye Rogue?

Char. Heaven forbid, Sir,— I said no such thing.

Sir Fran. Mercy on me! What a Plague it is to have a Son of One and Twenty, who wants to Elbow one out of one's Life, to Edge himself into the Estate.

Enter Marplot.

Marpl. Egad he's here— I was afraid I had lost him: His Secret cou'd not be with his Father, his Wants are Publick there— Guardian,—your Servant *Charles*, I know by that sorrowful Countenance of thine. The old Man's Fist is as close as his strong Box— But I'll help thee—

Sir Fran. So: Here's another extravagant Coxcomb, that will spend his Fortune before he comes to't; but he shall pay swinging Interest, and so let the Fool go on— Well, what do's Necessity bring you too, Sir?

Marpl. You have hit it, Guardian— I want a Hundred Pound.

Sir Fran. For what?

Marpl. Po'gh, for a Hundred Things, I can't for my Life tell you for what.

Char. Sir, I suppose I have received all the Answer I am like to have.

Marpl. Oh, the Devil, if he gets out before me, I shall lose him agen.

Sir Fran. Ay, Sir, and you may be marching as soon as you please— I must see a Change in your Temper e'er you find one in mine.

Marpl. Pray, Sir, dispatch me; the Money, Sir, I'm in mighty haste.

18*Sir Fran.* Fool, take this and go to the Cashier; I sha'n't be long plagu'd with thee.

(Gives him a Note.

Marpl. Devil take the Cashier, I shall certainly have *Charles* gone before I come back agen.

(Runs out.

Char. Well, Sir, I take my Leave— But remember, you Expose an only Son to all the Miseries of wretched Poverty, which too often lays the Plan for Scenes of Mischief.

Sir Fran. Stay, *Charles*, I have a sudden Thought come into my Head, may prove to thy Advantage.

Char. Ha, does he Relent?

Sir Fran. My Lady *Wrinkle*, worth Forty Thousand Pound, sets up for a Handsome young Husband; she prais'd thee t'other Day; tho' the Match-makers can get Twenty Guinea's for a sight of her, I can introduce thee for nothing.

Char. My Lady *Wrinkle*, Sir, why she has but one Eye.

Sir Fran. Then she'll see but half your Extravagance, Sir.

Char. Condemn me to such a piece of Deformity! Toothless, Dirty, Wry-neck'd, Hunch-back'd Hag.

Sir Fran. Hunch-back'd! so much the better, then she has a Rest for her Misfortunes; for thou wilt Load her swingingly. Now I warrant you think, this is no Offer of a Father; Forty Thousand Pound is nothing with you.

Char. Yes, Sir, I think it is too much; a young Beautiful Woman with half the Money wou'd be more agreeable. I thank you, Sir; but you Chose better for your self, I find.

12

Sir *Fran.* Out of my Doors, you Dog; you pretend to meddle with my Marriage, Sirrah.

Char. Sir, I obey: But—

Sir *Fran.* But me no Buts— Be gone, Sir: Dare to ask me for Money agen— Refuse Forty Thousand Pound! Out of my Doors, I say, without Reply.

(Exit Char.

Enter Servant.

Serv. One Sir *George Airy* enquires for you, Sir.

19**D2**

Enter Marplot *Running.*

Marpl. Ha? gone! Is *Charles* gone, Guardian?

Sir *Fran.* Yes; and I desire your wise Worship to walk after him.

Marpl. Nay, Egad, I shall Run, I tell you but that. Ah, Pox of the Cashier for detaining me so long, where the Devil shall I find him now. I shall certainly lose this Secret.

(Exit, hastily.

Sir *Fran.* What is the Fellow distracted?— Desire Sir *George* to walk up— Now for a Tryal of Skill that will make me Happy, and him a Fool: Ha, ha, ha, in my Mind he looks like an Ass already.

Enter Sir George.

Sir *Fran.* Well, Sir *George*, Dee ye hold in the same Mind? or wou'd you Capitulate? Ha, ha, ha: Look, here are the Guinea's,*(Chinks them.)* Ha, ha, ha.

Sir *Geo.* Not if they were twice the Sum, Sir *Francis.* Therefore be brief, call in the Lady, and take your Post—if she's a Woman, and, not seduc'd by Witchcraft to this old Rogue, I'll make his Heart ake; for if she has but one Grain of Inclination about her, I'll vary a Thousand Shapes, but find it.

(Aside.

Enter Mirand.

Sir *Fran.* Agreed—*Miranda.* There Sir *George*, try your Fortune,*(Takes out his Watch.)*

Sir *Geo.*

So from the Eastern Chambers breaks the Sun,
Dispels the Clouds, and gilds the Vales below.

(Salutes her.

Sir *Fran.* Hold, Sir, Kissing was not in our Agreement.

Sir *Geo.* Oh! That's by way of Prologue:— Prithee, Old Mammon, to thy Post.

Sir *Fran.* Well, young *Timon*, 'tis now 4 exactly; one Hour, remember is your utmost Limit, not a Minute more.

(Retires to the bottom of the Stage.

Sir *Geo.* Madam, whether you will Excuse or Blame my Love, the Author of this rash Proceeding depends upon your Pleasure, as also the Life of your Admirer; your 20sparkling Eyes speak a Heart susceptible of Love; your Vivacity a Soul too delicate to admit the Embraces of decay'd Mortality.

Miran. (Aside.) Oh, that I durst speak—

Sir *Geo.* Shake off this Tyrant *Guardian*'s Yoke, assume your self, and dash his bold aspiring Hopes; the Deity of his Desires, is Avarice; a Heretick in Love, and ought to be banish'd by the Queen of Beauty. See, Madam, a faithful Servant kneels and begs to be admitted in the Number of your Slaves.

(Miranda gives him her Hand to Raise him.

Sir *Fran.* I wish I cou'd hear what he says now. *(Running up.)*Hold, hold, hold, no Palming, that's contrary to Articles—

Sir *Geo.* Death, Sir, Keep your Distance, or I'll write another Article in your Guts.

(Lays his Hand to his Sword.

Sir *Fran. (Going back.)* A Bloody-minded Fellow!—

Sir *Geo.* Not Answer me! Perhaps she thinks my Address too Grave: I'll be more free— Can you be so Unconscionable, Madam, to let me say all these fine things to you without one single Compliment in Return? View me well, am I not a proper Handsome Fellow, ha? Can you prefer that old, dry, wither'd, sapless Log of Sixty-five, to the vigorous, gay, sprightly Love of Twenty-four? With Snoring only he'll awake thee, but I with Ravishing Delight wou'd make thy Senses Dance in Consort with the Joyful Minutes—ha? not yet, sure she is Dumb— Thus wou'd I steal and touch thy Beauteous Hand, *(Takes bold of her Hand)*till by degrees I reach'd thy snowy Breasts, then Ravish Kisses thus,

(Embraces her in Extasie.

Miran. (Strugles and flings from him.) Oh Heavens! I shall not be able to contain my self.

(Aside.

13

Sir *Fran.* *(Running up with his Watch in his Hand.)* Sure she did not speak to him— There's Three Quarters of the Hour gone, Sir*George*— Adod, I don't like those close Conferences—

Sir *Geo.* More Interruptions— You will have it, Sir.

(Lays his Hand to his Sword.

21Sir *Fran.* *(Going back.)* No, no, you shan't have her neither.

(Aside.

Sir *Geo.* Dumb still—sure this old Dog has enjoyn'd her Silence; I'll try another way— I must conclude, Madam, that in Compliance to your Guardian's Humour, you refuse to answer me— Consider the Injustice of his Injunction. This single Hour cost me a Hundred Pound—and wou'd you answer me, I cou'd purchase the 24 so: However, Madam, you must give me leave to make the best Interpretation I can for my Money, and take the Indication of your Silence for the secret Liking of my Person: Therefore, Madam, I will instruct you how to keep your Word inviolate to Sir *Francis*, and yet Answer me to every Question: As for Example, When I ask any thing, to which you wou'd Reply in the Affirmative, gently Nod your Head—thus; and when in the Negative thus; *(Shakes his Head.)* and in the doubtful a tender Sigh, thus

(Sighs.

Miran. How every Action charms me—but I'll fit him for Signs I warrant him.

(Aside.

Sir *Fran.* Ha, ha, ha, ha, poor Sir *George*, Ha, ha, ha, ha.

(Aside.

Sir *Geo.* Was it by his desire that you are Dumb, Madam, to all that I can say?

Miran. *(Nods.)*

Sir *Geo.* Very well! she's tractable I find— And is it possible that you can love him? Miraculous! *(*Miran. *Nods.)* Pardon the bluntness of my Questions, for my Time is short; may I not hope to supplant him in your Esteem? *(*Miran. *Sighs.)* Good! she answers me as I could wish— You'll not consent to marry him then?*(*Miran. *Sighs.)* How, doubtful in that— Undone again— Humph! but that may proceed from his Power to keep her out of her Estate till Twenty Five; I'll try that— Come, Madam, I cannot think you hesitate in this Affair out of any Motive, but your Fortune— Let him keep it till those few Years are expir'd; make me Happy with your Person, let him enjoy your Wealth—*(*Miran. *holds up her Hands.)* Why, 22what Sign is that now? Nay, nay, Madam, except you observe my Lesson, I can't understand your meaning—

Sir *Fran.* What a Vengeance, are they talking by Signs, 'ad I may be fool'd here; what do you mean, Sir *George?*

Sir *Geo.* To Cut your Throat if you dare Mutter another Syllable.

Sir *Fran.* Od! I wish he were fairly out of my House.

Sir *Geo.* Pray, Madam, will you answer me to the Purpose?*(*Miran. *shakes her Head, and points to Sir* Francis.*)* What! does she mean she won't answer me to the purpose, or is she afraid yon' old Cuff should understand her Signs?— Aye, it must be that, I perceive, Madam, you are too apprehensive of the Promise you have made to follow my Rules; therefore I'll suppose your Mind and answer for you— First, for my self, Madam, that I am in Love with you is an infallible Truth. Now for you: *(Turns on her side.)*Indeed, Sir, and may I believe it— As certainly, Madam, as that 'tis Day light, or that I Die if you persist in Silence— Bless me with the Musick of your Voice, and raise my Spirits to their proper Heaven: Thus low let me intreat; e'er I'm oblig'd to quit this Place, grant me some Token of a favourable Reception to keep my Hopes alive.*(Arises hastily turns of her side.)* Rise, Sir, and since my Guardian's Presence will not allow me Privilege of Tongue, Read that and rest assured you are not indifferent to me. *(Offers her a Letter.)* Ha! right Woman! But no *(She strikes it down.)* matter I'll go on.

Sir *Fran.* Ha! what's that a Letter— Ha, ha, ha, thou art baulk'd.

Miran. The best Assurance I ever saw—

(Aside.

Sir *Geo.* Ha? a Letter, Oh! let me Kiss it with the same Raptures that I would do the dear Hand that touch'd it. *(Opens it.)* Now for a quick Fancy and a long *Extempore*— What's here? *(Reads.)*"Dear, Sir *George*, this Virgin Muse I consecrate to you, which when it has receiv'd the Addition of your Voice, 'twill Charm me into Desire of Liberty to Love, which you, and only you can 23fix." My Angel! Oh you transport me! *(Kisses the Letter.)* And see the Power of your Command; the God of Love has set the Verse already; the flowing Numbers Dance into a Tune, and I'm inspir'd with a Voice to sing it.

Miran. I'm sure thou art inspir'd with Impudence enough.

Sir *Geo.* *(Sings.)*

Great Love inspire him;

Say I admire him.

Give me the Lover

14

That can discover
Secret Devotion
from silent Motion;
Then don't betray me,
But hence convey me.

    Sir *Geo. (Taking hold of* Miranda.*)* With all my Heart, this Moment let's
Retire. *(Sir* Francis *coming up hastily.)*

    Sir *Fran.* The Hour is expir'd, Sir, and you must take your leave. There, my Girl, there's the
Hundred Pound which thou hast won, go, I'll be with you presently, Ha, ha, ha, ha.

(Exit Miranda.

    Sir *Geo.* Ads Heart, Madam, you won't leave me just in the Nick, will you?

    Sir *Fran.* Ha, ha, ha, she has nick'd you, Sir *George*, I think, Ha, ha, ha: Have you any more
Hundred Pounds to throw away upon Courtship, Ha, ha, ha.

    Sir *Geo.* He, he, he, he, a Curse of your fleering Jests— Yet, however ill I succeeded, I'll
venture the same Wager, she does not value thee a spoonful of Snuff— Nay more, though you
enjoyn'd her Silence to me, you'll never make her speak to the Purpose with your self.

    Sir *Fran.* Ha, ha, ha, did not I tell thee thou would'st repent thy Money? Did not I say she
hated young Fellow's, Ha, ha, ha.

    Sir *Geo.* And I'm positive she's not in Love with Age.

    Sir *Fran.* Ha, ha, no matter for that, Ha, ha, she's not taken with your Youth, nor your
Rhetorick to boot, ha, ha.

    Sir *Geo.* Whate'er her Reasons are for disliking a me, I am certain she can be taken with
nothing about thee.

    24Sir *Fran.* Ha, ha, ha; how he swells with Envy!— Poor Man, poor Man— Ha, ha; I must
beg your Pardon, Sir *George, Miranda* will be Impatient to have her share of Mirth: Verily we shall
Laugh at thee most Egregiously; Ha, ha, ha.

    Sir *Geo.* With all my Heart, faith—I shall Laugh in my Turn too— For if you dare marry
her old *Belzebub,* you would be Cuckolded most Egregiously; Remember that, and Tremble—
She that to Age her Beauteous Self resigns,
Shows witty Management for close Designs.
Then if thou'rt grac'd with fair Miranda*'s Bed,*
Actæon*'s Horns she Means, shall Crown thy Head.*

(Exit.

    Sir *Fran.* Ha, ha, ha; he is mad.
These fluttering Fops imagine they can Wind,
Turn, and Decoy to Love, all Women-kind:
But here's a Proof of Wisdom in my Charge,
Old Men are Constant, Young Men live at Large.
The Frugal Hand can Bills at Sight defray,
When he that Lavish is, has Nought to pay.

(Exit.

S C E N E Changes to Sir Jealous Traffick's House.

Enter Sir Jealous, Isabinda; Patch following.

    Sir *Jeal.* What in the Balcone agen, notwithstanding my positive Commands to the
contrary!— Why don't you write a Bill upon your Forehead, to show Passengers there's
something to be Let—

    Isab. What harm can there be in a little fresh Air, Sir?

    Sir *Jeal.* Is your Constitution so hot, Mistriss, that it wants cooling, ha? Apply the
Virtuous *Spanish* Rules, banish your Tast, and Thoughts of Flesh, feed upon Roots, and quench
your Thirst with Water.

    Isab. That, and a close Room, wou'd certainly make me die of the Vapours.

    25ESir *Jeal.* No, Mistriss, 'tis your High-fed, Lusty, Rambling, Rampant Ladies—that are
troubl'd with the Vapours; 'tis your Ratifia, Persico, Cynamon, Citron, and Spirit of Clary, cause
such Swi—m—ing in the Brain, that carries many a Guinea full-tide to the Doctor. But you are
not to be Bred this way; No Galloping abroad, no receiving Visits at home; for in our loose
Country, the Women are as dangerous as the Men.

    Patch. So I told her, Sir; and that it was not Decent to be seen in a Balcone— But she
threaten'd to slap my Chaps, and told me, I was her Servant, not her Governess.

    Sir *Jeal.* Did she so? But I'll make her to know, that you are her*Duenna*: Oh that
incomparable Custom of *Spain!* why here's no depending upon old Women in my Country—for
they are as Wanton at Eighty, as a Girl of Eighteen; and a Man may as safely trust to *Asgill's*
Translation, as to his great Grand-Mother's not marrying agen.

15

Isab. Or to the *Spanish* Ladies Veils, and *Duenna's,* for the Safeguard of their Honour.

Sir Jeal. Dare to Ridicule the Cautious Conduct of that wise Nation, and I'll have you Lock'd up this Fortnight, without a Peephole.

Isab. If we had but the Ghostly Helps in *England,* which they have in *Spain,* I might deceive you if you did,— Sir, 'tis not the Restraint, but the Innate Principles, secures the Reputation and Honour of our Sex— Let me tell you, Sir, Confinement sharpens the Invention, as want of Sight strengthens the other Senses, and is often more Pernicious than the Recreation innocent Liberty allows.

Sir Jeal. Say you so, Mistress, who the Devil taught you the Art of Reasoning? I assure you, they must have a greater Faith than I pretend to, that can think any Woman innocent who requires Liberty. Therefore, *Patch,* to your Charge I give her; Lock her up till I come back from Change: I shall have some sauntring Coxcomb, with nothing but a Red Coat and a Feather, think, by Leaping into her Arms, to Leap into my Estate— But I'll prevent them, she shall be only Signeur *Babinetto's.*

26*Patch.* Really, Sir, I wish you wou'd employ any Body else in this Affair; I lead a Life like a Dog with obeying your Commands. Come, Madam, will you please to be Lock'd up.

Isab. Ay, to enjoy more Freedom than he is aware of. *(Aside.)*

(Exit with Patch.

Sir Jeal. I believe this Wench is very true to my Interest: I am happy I met with her, if I can but keep my Daughter from being blown upon till Signeur *Babinetto* arrives; who shall marry her as soon as he comes, and carry her to *Spain* as soon as he has marry'd her; she has a pregnant Wit, and I'd no more have her an *English* Wife, than the Grand Signior's Mistress.

(Exit.

Enter Whisper.

Whisp. So, I see Sir *Jealous* go out; where shall I find Mrs. *Patch* now.

Enter Patch.

Patch. Oh Mr. *Whisper,* my Lady saw you out at the Window, and order'd me to bid you fly, and let your Master know she's now alone.

Whisp. Hush, Speak softly; I go, go: But hark'e Mrs. *Patch,* shall not you and I have a little Confabulation, when my Master and your Lady is engag'd?

Patch. Ay, Ay, Farewell.

(Goes in, and shuts the Door.

Re-enter Sir Jealous Traffick *meeting* Whisper.

Sir Jeal. Sure whil'st I was talking with Mr. *Tradewell,* I heard my Door clap. *(Seeing* Whisper.*)* Ha! a Man lurking about my House; who do you want there, Sir?

Whisp. Want—want, a pox, Sir *Jealous!* what must I say now?—

(Aside.

Sir Jeal. Ay, want; have you a Letter or Message for any Body there?— O my Conscience, this is some He-Bawd—

Whisp. Letter or Message, Sir!

27E2*Sir Jeal.* Ay, Letter or Message, Sir.

Whisp. No, not I, Sir.

Sir Jeal. Sirrah, Sirrah, I'll have you set in the Stocks, if you don't tell me your Business immediately.

Whisp. Nay, Sir, my Business—is no great matter of Business neither; and yet 'tis Business of Consequence too.

Sir Jeal. Sirrah, don't trifle with me.

Whisp. Trifle, Sir, have you found him, Sir?

Sir Jeal. Found what, you Rascal.

Whisp. Why *Trifle* is the very Lap-Dog my Lady lost, Sir; I fancy'd I see him run into this House. I'm glad you have him— Sir, my Lady will be over-joy'd that 1 have found him.

Sir Jeal. Who is your Lady Friend?

Whisp. My Lady Love-puppy, Sir.

Sir Jeal. My Lady Love-puppy! then prithee carry thy self to her, for I know no other Whelp that belongs to her; and let me catch ye no more Puppy-hunting about my Doors, lest I have you prest into the Service, Sirrah.

Whisp. By no means, Sir— Your humble Servant; I must watch whether he goes, or no, before I can tell my Master.

(Exit.

Sir Jeal. This Fellow has the Officious Leer of a Pimp; and I half suspect a Design, but I'll be upon them before they think on me, I warrant 'em.

(Exit.

16

SCENE Charles's *Lodging*.
Enter Charles *and* Marplot.

Char. Honest *Marplot*, I thank thee for this Supply; I expect my Lawyer with a Thousand Pound I have order'd him to take up, and then you shall be Repaid.

Marpl. Pho, pho, no more of that: Here comes Sir *George Airy*—

Enter Sir George.

Cursedly out of Humour at his Disappointment; see how he looks! Ha, ha, ha.

28Sir *Geo.* Ah, *Charles*, I am so humbled in my Pretensions to Plots upon Women, that I believe I shall never have Courage enough to attempt a Chamber-maid agen—I'll tell thee.

Char. Ha, ha; I'll spare you the Relation by telling you— Impatient to know your Business with my Father, when I saw you Enter, I slipt back into the next Room, where I overheard every Syllable.

Sir Geo. That I said— But I'll be hang'd if you heard her Answer—. But prithee tell me, *Charles*, is she a Fool?

Char. I ne'er suspected her for one; but *Marplot* can inform you better, if you'll allow him a Judge.

Marpl. A Fool! I'll justifie she has more Wit than all the rest of her Sex put together; why she'll Rally me, till I han't one word to say for my self.

Char. A mighty Proof of her Wit truly—

Marpl. There must be some Trick in't, Sir *George*; Egad I'll find it out if it cost me the Sum you paid for't.

Sir Geo. Do and Command me—

Marpl. Enough, let me alone to Trace a Secret.—

Enter Whisper, *and speaks aside to his Master.*

The Devil! *Whisper* here agen, that Fellow never speaks out; is this the same, or a new Secret? Sir *George*, won't you ask *Charles* what News *Whisper* brings?

Sir Geo. Not I, Sir; I suppose it does not relate to me.

Marpl. Lord, Lord, how little Curiosity some People have! Now my chief Pleasure lies in knowing every Body's Business.

Sir Geo. I fancy, *Charles*, thou hast some Engagement upon thy Hands: I have a little Business too. *Marplot*, if it falls in your way to bring me any Intelligence from *Miranda*, you'll find me at the Thatch'd House at Six—

Marpl. You do me much Honour.

Char. You guess right, Sir *George*, wish me Success.

Sir Geo. Better than attended me. *Adieu.*

(*Exit.*

Char. Marplot, you must Excuse me.—

29*Marpl.* Nay, nay, what need of any Excuse amongst Friends! I'll go with you.

Char. Indeed you must not.

Marpl. No, then I suppose 'tis a Duel, and I will go to secure ye.

Char. Secure me, why you won't fight.

Marpl. What then! I can call People to part ye.

Char. Well, but it is no Duel, Consequently no Danger. Therefore prithee be Answer'd.

Marpl. What is't a Mistress then?— Mum— You know I can be silent upon occasion.

Char. I wish you cou'd be Civil too: I tell you, You neither Must nor Shall go with me. Farewel.

(*Exit.*

Marpl. Why then— I Must and Will follow you.

Exit.

The End of the Second Act.
ACT the Third
Enter Charles.

Char.

WELL, here's the House, which holds the Lovely Prize quiet and serene; here no noisie Footmen throng to tell the World, that Beauty dwells within; no Ceremonious Visit makes the Lover wait; no Rival to give my Heart a Pang; who wou'd not scale the Window at Midnight without fear of the Jealous Father's Pistol, rather than fill up the Train of a Coquet, where every Minute he is jostled out of Place. *(Knocks softly.)* Mrs. *Patch*, Mrs. *Patch.*

Enter Patch.

Patch. Oh, are you come, Sir? All's safe.

Char. So in, in then.

30

Enter Marplot.

Marpl. There he goes: Who the Devil lives here? Except I can find out that, I am as far from knowing his Business as ever; gad I'll watch, it may be a Bawdy-House, and he may have his Throat cut; if there shou'd be any Mischief, I can make Oath, he went in. Well, *Charles*, in spight of your Endeavour to keep me out of the Secret; I may save your Life, for ought I know: At that Corner I'll plant my self; there I shall see whoever goes in, or comes out. Gad, I love Discoveries.

(Exit.

SCENE *Draws.* Charles, Isabinda, *and* Patch.

Isab. Patch, look out sharp; have a care of Dad.

Patch. I warrant you.

(Exit.

Isab. Well, Sir, if I may judge your Love by your Courage, I ought to believe you sincere; for you venture into the Lyons Den when you come to see me.

Char. If you'd consent whilst the furious Beast is abroad, I'd free you from the Reach of his Paws.

Isab. That wou'd be but to avoid one Danger, by running into another; like the poor Wretches, who fly the Burning Ship, and meet their Fate in the Water. Come, come, *Charles*, I fear if I consult my Reason, Confinement and Plenty is better than Liberty and Starving. I know you'd make the Frolick pleasing for a little time, by Saying and Doing a World of tender things; but when our small Substance is once Exhausted, and a Thousand Requisits for Life are Wanting; Love, who rarely dwells with Poverty, wou'd also fail us.

Char. Faith, I fancy not; methinks my Heart has laid up a Stock will last for Life; to back which, I have taken a Thousand Pound upon my Uncle's Estate; that surely will support us, till one of our Fathers relent.

Isab. There's no trusting to that my Friend, I doubt your Father will carry his Humour to the Grave, and mine till he sees me settled in *Spain.*

Char. And can ye then cruelly Resolve to stay till that 31curs'd *Don*arrives, and suffer that Youth, Beauty, Fire and Wit, to be sacrific'd to the Arms of a dull *Spaniard*, to be Immur'd and forbid the Sight of any thing that's Humane.

Isab. No, when it comes to the Extremity, and no Stratagem can Relieve us, thou shalt List for a Soldier, and I'll carry thy Knapsack after thee.

Char. Bravely Resolv'd; the World cannot be more Savage than our Parents, and Fortune generally assists the Bold; therefore Consent now: Why shou'd we put it to a future Hazard? who knows when we shall have another Opportunity?

Isab. Oh, you have your Ladder of Ropes, I suppose, and the Closet Window stands just where it did; and if you han't forgot to write in Characters, *Patch* will find a way for our Assignations. Thus much of the *Spanish* Contrivance, my Father's Severity has taught me, I thank him; tho' I hate the Nation, I admire their Management in these Affairs.

Enter Patch.

Patch. Oh, Madam, I see my Master coming up the Street.

Char. Oh the Devil, wou'd I had my Ladder now; I thought you had not expected him till Night; why, why, why, why; what shall I do, Madam?

Isab. Oh, for Heaven's sake! don't go that way, you'll meet him full in the Teeth: Oh unlucky Moment!—

Char. Adsheart, can you shut me into no Cupboard, Ram me into no Chest, ha?

Patch. Impossible, Sir, he Searches every Hole in the House.

Isab. Undone for ever! if he sees you, I shall never see you more.

Patch. I have thought on't: Run you to your Chamber, Madam; and Sir, come you along with me, I'm certain you may easily get down from the Balcone.

Char. My Life, *Adieu*— Lead on, Guide.

(Exit.

Isab. Heaven preserve him.

(Exit.

32

S C E N E Changes to the Street.

Enter Sir Jealous, *with* Marplot *behind him.*

Sir Jeal. I don't know what's the matter; but I have a strong Suspicion, all is not right within; that Fellow's sauntring about my Door, and his Tale of a Puppy, had the Face of a Lye, methought. By St. *Jago*, if I shou'd find a Man in the House, I'd make Mince-Meat of him—

Marpl. Ah, poor *Charles*—ha? Agad he is old— I fancy I might bully him, and make *Charles* have an Opinion of my Courage.

Sir Jeal. My own Key shall let me in; I'll give them no Warning.

18

Marpl. What's that you say, Sir.

(*Feeling for his Key.*

Sir Jeal. What's that to you, Sir.

(*Going up to Sir* Jealous.

(*Turns quick upon him.*

Marpl. Yes, 'tis to me, Sir; for the Gentleman you threaten is a very honest Gentleman. Look to't, for if he comes not as safe out of your House, as he went in, I have half a Dozen *Mirmidons* hard-by shall beat it about your Ears.

Sir Jeal. Went in; what is he in then? Ah! a Combination to undo me— I'll *Mirmidon* you, ye Dog you— Thieves, Thieves.

(*Beat's* Marplot *all this while he cries* Thieves.

Marpl. Murder, Murder; I was not in your House, Sir.

Enter Servant.

Serv. What's the matter, Sir?

Sir Jeal. The Matter, Rascals? Have you let a Man into my House; but I'll flea him Alive, follow me, I'll not leave a Mousehole unsearch'd; if I find him, by St. *Jago,* I'll Equip him for the *Opera.*

(*Exit.*

Marpl. A Duce of his Cane, there's no trusting to Age—what shall I do to Relieve *Charles!* Egad, I'll raise the Neighbourhood— Murder, Murder— (Charles *drops down upon him from the Balcone.*) *Charles* faith I'm glad to see thee safe out, with all my Heart.

Char. A Pox of your Bawling: How the Devil came you here?

33F*Marpl.* Here, gad I have done you a piece of Service; I told the old Thunderbolt, that the Gentleman that was gone in was—

Char. Was it you that told him, Sir? (*Laying hold of him.*)Z'death, I cou'd crush thee into Atoms.

(*Exit* Charles.

Marpl. What will you choak me for my Kindness?—will my Enquiring Soul never leave Searching into other Peoples Affairs, till it gets squeez'd out of my Body? I dare not follow him now, for my Blood, he's in such a Passion— I'll to *Miranda;* if I can discover ought that may oblige Sir *George,* it may be a means to Reconcile me agen to *Charles.*

(*Exit.*

Enter Sir Jealous *and* Servants.

Sir Jeal. Are you sure you have search'd every where?

Serv. Yes, from the Top of the House to the Bottom.

Sir Jeal. Under the Beds, and over the Beds?

Serv. Yes, and in them too, but found no Body, Sir.

Sir Jeal. Why, what cou'd this Rogue mean?

Enter Isabinda *and* Patch.

Patch. Take Courage, Madam, I saw him safe out.

(*Aside to* Isab.

Isab. Bless me! what's the matter, Sir?

Sir Jeal. You know best— Pray where's the Man that was here just now?

Isab. What Man, Sir? I saw none!

Patch. Nor I, by the Trust you repose in me; do you think I wou'd let a Man come within these Doors, when you were absent?

Sir Jeal. Ah *Patch,* she may be too cunning for thy Honesty; the very Scout that he had set to give Warning discover'd it to me—and threaten'd me with half a Dozen *Mirmidons*— But I think I maul'd the Villain. These Afflictions you draw upon me, Mistress!

Isab. Pardon me, Sir, 'tis your own Ridiculous Humour draws you into these Vexations, and gives every Fool pretence to banter you.

Sir Jeal. No, 'tis your Idle Conduct, your Coquetish Flurting into the Balcone— Oh with what Joy shall I resign thee into the Arms of Don *Diego Babinetto!*

34*Isab.* And with what Industry shall I avoid him!

(*Aside.*

Sir Jeal. Certainly that Rogue had a Message from some body or other; but being baulk'd by my coming, popt that Sham upon me. Come along, ye Sots, let's see if we can find the Dog again. *Patch,* lock her up; D'ye hear?

(*Exit with Servants.*

Patch. Yes, Sir—ay, walk till your Heels ake, you'll find no Body, I promise you.

Isab. Who cou'd that Scout be, which he talks of?

Patch. Nay, I can't imagine, without it was *Whisper.*

19

Isab. Well, dear *Patch*, let's employ all our Thoughts how to escape this horrid Don *Diego*, my very Heart sinks at his Terrible Name.

Patch. Fear not, Madam, Don *Carlo* shall be the Man, or I'll lose the Reputation of Contriving, and then what's a Chambermaid good for?

Isab. Say'st thou so, my Girl: Then—

Let Dad be Jealous, multiply his Cares,
While Love instructs me to avoid the Snares;
I'll, spight of all his Spanish Caution, show
How much for Love a British Maid can do.

(Exit.

SCENE *Sir* Francis Gripe's *House.*

Sir Francis *and* Miranda *meeting.*

Miran. Well, *Gardee*, how did I perform my Dumb Scene?

Sir Fran. To Admiration— Thou dear little Rogue, let me buss thee for it: Nay, adod, I will, *Chargee*, so muzle, and tuzle, and hug thee; I will, I faith, I will.

(Hugging and Kissing her.

Miran. Nay, *Gardee*, don't be so lavish; who wou'd Ride Post, when the Journey lasts for Life?

Sir Fran. Ah wag, ah wag— I'll buss thee agen for that.

Miran. Faugh! how he stinks of Tobacco! what a delicate Bedfellow I shou'd have!

(Aside.

Sir Fran. Oh I'm Transported! When, when, my Dear, wilt thou Convince the World of thy Happy Day? when shall we marry, ha?

35F2*Miran.* There's nothing wanting but your Consent, Sir *Francis.*

Sir Fran. My Consent! what do's my Charmer mean?

Miran. Nay, 'tis only a Whim: But I'll have every thing according to form— Therefore when you sign an Authentick Paper, drawn up by an able Lawyer, that I have your Leave to marry, the next Day makes me yours, *Gardee.*

Sir Fran. Ha, ha, ha, a Whim indeed! why is it not Demonstration I give my Leave when I marry thee.

Miran. Not for your Reputation, *Gardee*; the malicious World will be apt to say, you trick'd me into Marriage, and so take the Merit from my Choice. Now I will have the Act my own, to let the idle Fops see how much I prefer a Man loaded with Years and Wisdom.

Sir Fran. Humph! Prithee leave out Years, *Chargee*, I'm not so old, as thou shalt find: Adod, I'm young; there's a Caper for ye.

(Jumps.

Miran. Oh never excuse it, why I like you the better for being old— But I shall suspect you don't love me, if you Refuse me this Formality.

Sir Fran. Not Love thee, *Chargee*! Adod I do love thee better than, than, than, better than— what shall I say? Egad, better than Money, I faith I do—

Miran. That's false I'm sure *(Aside.)* To prove it do this then.

Sir Fran. Well, I will do it, *Chargee*, provided I bring a License at the same time.

Miran. Ay, and a Parson too, if you please; Ha, ha, ha, I can't help Laughing to think how all the young Coxcombs about Town will be mortify'd when they hear of our Marriage.

Sir Fran. So they will, so they will; Ha, ha, ha.

Miran. Well, I fancy I shall be so happy with my *Gardee!*

Sir Fran. If wearing Pearls and Jewels, or eating Gold, as the old Saying is, can make thee happy, thou shalt be so, my Sweetest, my Lovely, my Charming, my—verily I know not what to call thee.

Miran. You must know, *Gardee*, that I am so eager to have this Business concluded, that I have employ'd my Womans Brother, who is a Lawyer in the *Temple*, to settle Matters 36just to your Liking, you are to give your Consent to my Marriage, which is to your self, you know: But Mum, you must take up notice of that. So then I will, that is, with your Leave, put my Writings into his Hands; then to Morrow we come slap upon them with a Wedding, that no body thought on; by which you seize me and my Estate, and I suppose make a Bonfire of your own Act and Deed.

Sir Fran. Nay, but *Chargee*, if—

Miran. Nay, *Gardee*, no Ifs— Have I refus'd three *Northern* Lords, two *British* Peers, and half a score Knights, to have you put in your Ifs?—

Sir Fran. So thou hast indeed, and I will trust to thy Management. Od, I'm all of a Fire.

Miran. 'Tis a wonder the dry Stubble does not blaze.

Enter Marplot.

Sir Fran. How now! who sent for you, Sir? What's the Hundred Pound gone already?

Marpl. No, Sir, I don't want Money now.

Sir Fran. No, that's a Miracle! But there's one thing you want, I'm sure.

Marpl. Ay, what's that, *Guardian?*

Sir Fran. Manners, what had I no Servants without?

Marpl. None that cou'd do my Business, *Guardian,* which is at present with this Lady.

Miran. With me, Mr. *Marplot!* what is it, I beseech you?

Sir Fran. Ay, Sir, what is it? any thing that relates to her may be deliver'd to me.

Marpl. I deny that.

Miran. That's more than I do, Sir.

Marpl. Indeed, Madam, why then to proceed: Fame says, that you and my most Conscionable *Guardian* here, design'd, contriv'd, plotted and agreed to chouse a very civil, honourable, honest Gentleman, out of a Hundred Pound.

Miran. That I contrived it!

Marpl. Ay you— You said never a Word against it, so far you are Guilty.

Sir Fran. Pray tell that civil, honourable, honest Gentleman, 37that if he has any more such Sums to fool away, they shall be received like the last; Ha, ha, ha, ha, chous'd, quotha! But hark ye, let him know at the same time, that if he dare to report I trick'd him of it, I shall recommend a Lawyer to him shall shew him a Trick for twice as much; D'ye hear, tell him that.

Marpl. So, and this is the way you use a Gentleman, and my Friend.

Miran. Is the Wretch thy Friend?

Marpl. The Wretch! Look ye, Madam, don't call Names; Egad I won't take it.

Miran. Why you won't beat me, will you? Ha, ha.

Marpl. I don't know whether I will or no.

Sir Fran. Sir, I shall make a Servant shew you out at the Window if you are sawcy.

Marpl. I am your most humble Servant, *Guardian*; I design to go out the same way I came in. I wou'd only ask this Lady, if she do's not think in her Soul Sir *George Airy* is not a fine Gentleman.

Miram. He Dresses well.

Sir Fran. Which is chiefly owing to his Taylor, and *Valet de Chamber.*

Miran. And if you allow that a proof of his being a fine Gentleman, he is so.

Marpl. The judicious part of the World allow him Wit, Courage, Gallantry and Management; tho' I think he forfeited that Character, when he flung away a Hundred Pound upon your Dumb Ladyship.

Sir Fran. Does that gaul him? Ha, ha, ha.

Miran. So, Sir *George* remaining in deep Discontent, has sent you his trusty Squire, to utter his Complaint: Ha, ha, ha.

Marpl. Yes, Madam; and you, like a cruel, hard-hearted Jew, value it no more—than I wou'd your Ladyship, were I Sir *George*, you, you, you—

Miran. Oh, don't call Names. I know you love to be employ'd, and I'll oblige you; and you shall carry him a Message from me.

38*Marpl.* According as I like it: What is it?

Miran. Nay, a kind one you may be sure— First tell him, I have chose this Gentleman to have, and to hold, and so forth.

(Clapping her Hand into Sir Francis's.

Sir Fran. Oh the dear Rogue, how I dote on her!

(Aside.

Miran. And advise his Impertinence to trouble me no more, for I prefer Sir *Francis* for a Husband before all the Fops in the Universe.

Marpl. Oh Lord, Oh Lord! She's bewitch'd, that's certain; Here's a Husband for Eighteen— Here's a Shape— Here's Bones ratling in a Leathern Bag. *(Turning Sir* Francis *about.)* Here's Buckram, and Canvass, to scrub you to Repentance.

Sir Fran. Sirrah, my Cane shall teach you Repentance presently.

Marpl. No faith, I have felt its Twin-Brother from just such a wither'd Hand too lately.

Miran. One thing more, advise him to keep from the Garden Gate on the left Hand; for if he dares to saunter there, about the Hour of Eight, as he used to do, he shall be saluted with a Pistol or a Blunderbuss.

Sir Fran. Oh monstrous! why *Chargee*; did he use to come to the Garden Gate?

Miran. The Gardner describ'd just such another Man that always watch'd his coming out, and fain wou'd have bribed him for his Entrance—tell him he shall find a warm Reception if he comes this Night.

Marpl. Pistols and Blunderbusses! Egad, a warm Reception indeed; I shall take care to inform him of your Kindness, and advise him to keep farther off.

Miran. I hope he will understand my Meaning better, than to follow your Advice.

(Aside.

Sir *Fran.* Thou hast sign'd, seal'd, and ta'en Possession of my Heart; for ever, *Chargee*, Ha, ha, ha; and for you, Mr. Sauce-box, let me have no more of your Messages, if ever you design to inherit your Estate, Gentleman.

Marpl. Why there 'tis now. Sure I shall be out of your Clutches one Day.— Well, *Guardian*, I say no more; but if you be not as errant a Cuckold, as e're drove Bargain upon 39the Exchange, or paid Attendance to a Court; I am the Son of a Whetstone; and so your humble Servant.

(Exit.

Miran. Don't forget the Message; Ha, ha.

Sir *Fran.* I am so provok'd!—'tis well he's gone.

Miran. Oh mind him not, *Gardee*, but let's sign Articles, and then—

Sir *Fran.* And then— Adod, I believe I am Metamorphos'd; my Pulse beats high, and my Blood boils, methinks—

(Kissing and Hugging her.

Miran. Oh fye, *Gardee*, be not so violent; Consider the Market lasts all the Year— Well, I'll in and see if the Lawyer be come, you'll follow.

(Exit.

Sir *Fran.* Ay, to the World's End, my Dear. Well, *Franck*, thou art a lucky Fellow in thy old Age, to have such a delicate Morsel, and Thirty Thousand Pound in love with thee; I shall be the Envy of Batchelors, the Glory of Marry'd Men, and the Wonder of the Town. Some Guardians wou'd be glad to compound for part of the Estate, at dispatching an Heiress, but I engross the whole: *O! Mihi præteritos referet si Jupiter Annos.*

(Exit.

S C E N E *Changes to a Tavern; discovers Sir* George *and* Charles *with Wine before them, and* Whisper *waiting.*

Sir *Geo.* Nay, prithee don't be Grave, *Charles;* Misfortunes will happen: Ha, ha, ha, 'tis some Comfort to have a Companion in our Sufferings.

Char. I am only apprehensive for *Isabinda*, her Father's Humour is implacable; and how far his Jealousie may transport him to her Undoing, shocks my Soul to think.

Sir *Geo.* But since you escap'd undiscover'd by him, his Rage will quickly lash into a Calm, never fear it.

Char. But who knows what that unlucky Dog, *Marplot*, told him; nor can I imagine what brought him thither; that Fellow is ever doing Mischief; and yet, to give him his due, he never designs it. This is some Blundering Adventure, 40wherein he thought to shew his Friendship, as he calls it: A Curse on him.

Sir *Geo.* Then you must forgive him; what said he?

Char. Said! nay, I had more mind to cut his Throat, than hear his Excuses.

Sir *Geo.* Where is he?

Whisp. Sir, I saw him go into Sir *Francis Gripe*'s just now.

Char. Oh! then he is upon your Business, Sir *George*; a thousand to one, but he makes some Mistake there too.

Sir *Geo.* Impossible, without he huffs the Lady, and makes Love to Sir *Francis*.

Enter Drawer.

Draw. Mr. *Marplot* is below, Gentlemen, and desires to know if he may have Leave to wait upon ye.

Char. How civil the Rogue is when he has done a fault!

Sir *Geo.* Ho! Desire him to walk up. Prithee, *Charles*, throw off this Chagreen, and be good Company.

Char. Nay, hang him, I'm not angry with him. *Whisper*, fetch me Pen, Ink and Paper.

Whisp. Yes, Sir.

(Ex. Whisp.

Enter Marplot.

Char. Do but mark his sheepish Look, Sir *George*.

Marpl. Dear *Charles*, don't o'erwhelm a Man—already under insupportable Affliction. I'm sure I always intend to serve my Friends; but if my malicious Stars deny the Happiness, is the fault mine?

Sir *Geo.* Never mind him, Mr. *Marplot*, he is eat up with Spleen. But tell me, what says *Miranda?*

Marpl. Says—nay, we are all undone there too.

22

Char. I told you so; nothing prospers that he undertakes.

Marpl. Why can I help her having chose your Father for Better for Worse?

Char. So: There's another of Fortune's Strokes; I suppose I shall be Edg'd out of my Estate, with Twins every Year, let who will get 'em.

Sir *Geo.* What is the Woman really Possest?

41**G***Marpl.* Yes with the Spirit of Contradiction, she rail'd at you most prodigiously.

Sir *Geo.* That's no ill Sign.

Enter Whisper, *with Pen, Ink and Paper.*

Marpl. You'd say it was no good Sign, if you knew all.

Sir *Geo.* Why, prithee?

Marpl. Hark'e, Sir *George*, Let me warn you, pursue your old Haunt no more, it may be dangerous.

(Charles sits down to write.

Sir *Geo.* My old Haunt, what d'you mean?

Marpl. Why in short then, since you will have it, *Miranda* vows if you dare approach the Garden-Gate at Eight a Clock, as you us'd, you shall be saluted with a Blunderbuss, Sir. These were her Words; nay, she bid me tell you so too.

Sir *George*, Ha! The Garden-Gate at Eight, as I us'd to do! There must be a Meaning in this. Is there such a Gate, *Charles*?

Char. Yes, yes; it opens into the Park, I suppose her Ladyship has made many a Scamper through it.

Sir *Geo.* It must be an Assignation then. Ha, my Heart springs with Joy, 'tis a propitious Omen. My dear *Marplot*, let me embrace thee, thou art my Friend, my better Angel—

Marpl. What do you mean, Sir *George*?

Sir *Geo.* No matter what I mean. Here take a Bumper to the Garden-Gate, ye dear Rogue, you.

Marpl. You have Reason to be transported, Sir *George*; I have sav'd your Life.

Sir *Geo.* My Life! thou hast sav'd my Soul, Man. *Charles*, if thou do'st not pledge this Health, may'st thou never taste the Joys of Love.

Char. Whisper, be sure you take care how you deliver this *(gives him the Letter)* bring me the Answer to my Lodgings.

Whisp. I warrant you, Sir.

(Exit.

42*Marpl.* Whither does that Letter go?— Now dare I not ask for my Blood.

Char. Now I'm for you.

Sir *Geo.* To the Garden-Gate at the Hour of Eight, *Charles*, along, Huzza!

Char. I begin to conceive you.

Marpl. That's more than I do, Egad—to the Garden-Gate, Huzza,*(Drinks.)* But I hope you design to keep far enough off on't, Sir*George*.

Sir *Geo.* Ay, ay, never fear that; she shall see I despise her Frowns, let her use her Blunderbuss against the next Fool, she shan't reach me with the Smoak, I warrant her, Ha, ha, ha.

Marpl. Ah, *Charles*, if you cou'd receive a Disappointment thus *En Cavalier*, one shou'd have some comfort in being beat for you.

Char. The Fool comprehends nothing.

Sir *Geo.* Nor wou'd I have him; prithee take him along with thee.

Char. Enough: *Marplot*, you shall go home with me.

Marpl. I'm glad I'm well with him however. Sir *George*, yours. Egad, *Charles*, asking me to go home with him, gives me a shrewd suspicion there's more in the Garden-Gate, than I comprehend. Faith, I'll give him the drop, and away to *Guardians*, and find it out.

Sir *Geo.* I kiss both your Hands— And now for the Garden-Gate.

It's Beauty gives the Assignation there,
And Love too powerful grows t' admit of Fear.

(Exit.

The End of the Third Act.

43**G2**

ACT the Fourth.
S C E N E the Out-side of Sir *Jealous Traffick*'s House,
Patch peeping out of Door.
Enter Whisper.

Whisp.

HA, Mrs. *Patch*, this is a lucky Minute, to find you so readily, my Master dies with Impatience.

23

Patch. My Lady imagin'd so, and by her Orders I have been scouting this hour in search of you, to inform you that Sir *Jealous* has invited some Friends to Supper with him to Night, which gives an Opportunity to your Master to make use of his Ladder of Ropes: The Closet Window shall be open, and *Isabinda* ready to receive him; bid him come immediately.

Whisp. Excellent, He'll not disappoint I warrant him: But hold, I have a Letter here, which I'm to carry an Answer of: I can't think what Language the Direction is.

Patch. Pho, 'tis no Language, but a Character which the Lovers invented to avert Discovery: Ha, I hear my old Master coming down Stairs, it is impossible you shou'd have an Answer; away, and bid him come himself for that—begone we are ruined if you're seen, for he has doubl'd his Care since the last Accident.

Whisp. I go, I go.

[*Exit.*

Patch. There, go thou into my Pocket. [*Puts it besides, and it falls down.*] Now I'll up the back Stairs, lest I meet him. Well, a dexterous Chamber-maid is the Ladies best Utensil, I say.

[*Exit.*

Enter Sir Jealous *with a Letter in his Hand.*

Sir Jeal. So, this is some Comfort, this tells me that *Seignior Don Diego Babinetto* is safely arriv'd, he shall marry my Daughter the Minute he comes, ha. What's here [*takes up the Letter* Patch *drop'd*] a Letter! I don't know what to 44 make of the Superscription. I'll see what's within side, [*opens it*] humph; 'tis *Hebrew* I think. What can this mean. There must be some trick in it; this was certainly design'd for my Daughter, but I don't know that she can speak any Language but her Mother-Tongue. No matter for that, this may be one of Love's Hieroglyphicks, and I fancy I saw *Patch*'s Tail sweep by. That Wench may be a Slut, and instead of guarding my Honour, betray it; I'll find it out I'm resolv'd; who's there? What Answer did you bring from the Gentlemen I sent you to invite?

Serv. That they'd all wait of you, Sir, as I told you before, but I suppose you forget, Sir.

Sir Jeal. Did I so, Sir, but I shan't forget to break your Head, if any of 'em come, Sir.

Serv. Come, Sir, why did not you send me to desire their Company, Sir?

Sir Jeal. But I send you now to desire their Absence; say I have something extraordinary fallen out, which calls me abroad, contrary to Expectation, and ask their Pardon, and d'ye hear, send the Butler to me.

Serv. Yes, Sir.

[*Exit.*

Enter Butler.

Sir Jeal. If this Paper has a Meaning I'll find it. Lay the Cloath in my Daughter's Chamber, and bid the Cook send Supper thither presently.

Butl. Yes, Sir,—hey day, what's the Matter now?

[*Exit.*

Sir Jeal. He wants the Eyes of *Argus*, that has a young handsome Daughter in this Town, but my Comfort is, I shall not be troubl'd long with her. He that pretends to rule a Girl once in her Teens, had better be at Sea in a Storm, and would be in less Danger.

For let him do, or Counsel all he can,
She thinks and dreams of nothing else but Man.

[*Exit.*

45

S C E N E *Isabinda's* Chamber, *Isabinda* and *Patch.*

Isab. Are you sure, no Body saw you speak to *Whisper?*

Patch. Yes, very sure Madam, but I heard Sir *Jealous* coming down Stairs, so I clap'd this Letter into my Pocket.

(*Feels for the Letter.*

Isab. A Letter! give it me quickly.

Patch. Bless me! what's become on't— I'm sure I put it—

(*Searching still.*

Isab. Is it possible, thou could'st be so Careless— Oh! I'm undone for ever if it be lost.

Patch. I must have drop'd it upon the Stairs. But why are you so much alarm'd, if the worst happens no body can read it, Madam, nor find out whom it was design'd for.

Isab. If it falls into my Father's Hands the very Figure of a Letter will produce ill Consequences. Run and look for it upon the Stairs this Moment.

Patch. Nay, I'm sure it can be no where else.— (*As she's going out of the Door meets the Butler.*) How now, what do you want?

Butl. My Master order'd me to lay the Cloth here for his Supper.

Isab. Ruin'd past Redemption—

24

Patch. You mistake sure; what shall we do?

Isab. I thought he expected Company to Night— Oh! poor *Charles*— Oh! unfortunate *Isabinda*.

Butl. I thought so too Madam, but I suppose he has alter'd his Mind.

(*Lays the Cloth, and Exit.*

Isab. The Letter is the Cause; this heedless Action has undone me: Fly and fasten the Closet-window, which will give *Charles* notice to retire. Ha, my Father, oh! Confusion.

Enter Sir Jealous.

Sir Jeal. Hold, hold, *Patch*, whither are you going. I'll have no body stir out of the Room till after Supper.

Patch. Sir, I was only going to reach your easie Chair— Oh! wretched Accident!

46Sir *Jeal.* I'll have no body stir out of the Room. I don't want my easie Chair.

Isab. What will be the event of this?

(*Aside.*

Sir Jeal. Hark ye Daughter, do you know this Hand?

Isab. As I suspected— Hand do you call it, Sir? 'Tis some School-boy's Scraul.

Patch. Oh! Invention, thou Chamber-maid's best Friend, assist me.

(*Aside.*

Sir Jeal. Are you sure you don't understand it?

(*Patch. Feels in her Bosom, and shakes her Coats.*)

Isab. Do you understand it, Sir?

Sir Jeal. I wish I did.

Isab. Thank Heaven you do not. (*aside*) Then I know no more of it than you do indeed, Sir.

Patch. Oh Lord, Oh Lord, what have you done, Sir? Why the Paper is mine, I drop'd it out of my Bosom.

(*Snatching it from him.*

Sir Jeal. Ha! yours, Mistress.

Isab. What does she mean by owning it.

(*Aside.*

Patch. Yes, Sir, it is.

Sir Jeal. What is it? Speak.

Patch. Why, Sir, it is a Charm for the Tooth-ach— I have worn it this seven Year, 'twas given me by an Angel for ought I know, when I was raving with the Pain; for no body knew from whence he came, nor whither he went, he charg'd me never to open it, lest some dire Vengeance befal me, and Heaven knows what will be the Event. Oh! cruel Misfortune that I should drop it, and you should open it— If you had not open'd it—

Isab. Excellent Wench.

(*Aside.*

Sir Jeal. Pox of your Charms, and Whims for me, if that be all 'tis well enough; there, there, burn it, and I warrant you no Vengeance will follow.

Patch. So, all's right again thus far.

(*Aside.*

Isab. I would not lose *Patch* for the World— I'll take courage a little. (*aside*) Is this Usage for your Daughter, Sir, must my Virtue and Conduct be suspected? For every Trifle, you immure me like some dire Offender here, and deny me 47all Recreations which my Sex enjoy, and the Custom of the Country and Modesty allow; yet not content with that you make my Confinement more intolerable by your Mistrusts and Jealousies; wou'd I were dead, so I were free from this.

(*Weeps.*

Sir Jeal. To morrow rids you of this tiresome Load,—*Don Diego Babinetto* will be here, and then my Care ends and his begins.

Isab. Is he come then! Oh how shall I avoid this hated Marriage?

(*Aside.*

Enter Servants with Supper.

Sir Jeal. Come will you sit down?

Isab. I can't eat, Sir.

Patch. No, I dare swear he has given her Supper enough. I wish I cou'd get into the Closet—

(*Aside.*

Sir Jeal. Well, if you can't eat, then give me a Song whilst I do.

Isab. I have such a Cold I can scarce speak, Sir, much less sing. How shall I prevent *Charles* coming in.

25

Sir Jeal. I hope you have the Use of your Fingers, Madam. Play a Tune upon your *Spinnet*, whilst your Woman sings me a Song.

Patch. I'm as much out of Tune as my Lady, if he knew all.

(Aside.

Isab. I shall make excellent Musick.

(Sits down to play.

Patch. Really, Sir, I'm so frighted about your opening this Charm, that I can't remember one Song.

Sir Jeal. Pish, hang your Charm; come, come, sing any thing.

Patch. Yes, I'm likely to sing truly *(aside)* humph, humph, bless me, Sir, I cannot raise my Voice, my Heart pants so.

Sir Jeal. Why, what does your Heart pant so that you can't play neither? Pray what Key are you in, ha?

Patch. Ah, wou'd the Key was turn'd of you once.

(Aside.

Sir Jeal. Why don't you sing, I say!

Patch. When Madam has put her *Spinnet* in Tune, Sir, humph, humph.—

48*Isab.* I cannot play, Sir, whatever ails me.

(Rising.

Sir Jeal. Zounds sit down, and play me a Tune, or I'll break the *Spinnet* about your Ears.

Isab. What will become of me?

(Sits down and plays.

Sir Jeal. Come, Mistress.

(To Patch

Patch. Yes, Sir.

(Sings, but horribly out of Tune.

Sir Jeal. Hey, hey, why you are a top of the House, and you are down in the Cellar. What is the meaning of this? Is it on purpose to cross me, ha?

Patch. Pray Madam, take it a little lower, I cannot reach that Note—nor any Note I fear.

Isab. Well, begin— Oh! *Patch* we shall be discover'd.

Patch. I sink with the Apprehension, Madam,—humph, humph—

*(Sings)(*Charles *pulls open the Closet Door.*

Char. Musick and Singing

'Tis thus the bright Coelestial Court above,

Beguiles the Hours with Musick and with Love.

Death! her Father there, *(The Women shriek)* then I must fly—

(Exit into the Closet)

(Sir Jealous *rises up hastily, seeing* Charles *slip back into the Closet.*

Sir Jeal. Hell and Furies, a Man in the Closet—

Patch. Ah! a Ghost, a Ghost—he must not enter the Closet—

*(*Isabinda *throws her self down before the Closet-door as in a Sound.*

Sir Jeal. The Devil! I'll make a Ghost of him I warrant you.

(Strives to get by.

Patch. Oh hold, Sir, have a care, you'l tread upon my Lady— who waits there? Bring some Water: Oh! this comes of your opening the Charm: Oh, oh, oh, oh.

(Weeps aloud.

Sir Jeal. I'll Charm you, House-wife, here lies the Charm, that conjur'd this Fellow in I'm sure on't, come out you Rascal, do so: Zounds take her from the Door, or I'll spurn her from it, and break your Neck down Stairs.

Isab. Oh, oh, where am I— He's gone, I heard him leap down.

(Aside to Patch.

Patch. Nay, then let him enter—here, here Madam, smell to this; come give me your Hand; come nearer to the Window, the Air will do you good.

49H*Sir Jeal.* I wou'd she were in her Grave. Where are you, Sirrah, Villain, Robber of my Honour; I'll pull you out of your Nest.

(Goes into the Closet.

Patch. You'l be mistaken, old Gentleman, the Bird is flown.

Isab. I'm glad I have 'scap'd so well. I was almost dead in earnest with the Fright.

Re-enter Sir Jealous *out of the Closet.*

Sir Jeal. Whoever the Dog were he has escap'd out of the Window, for the Sash is up. But tho' he is got out of my Reach, you are not: And first Mrs. *Pandor*, with your Charms for Tooth-ach, get out of my House, go, troop; yet hold, stay, I'll see you out of my Doors my self, but I'll secure your Charge e'er I go.

Isab. What do you mean, Sir? Was she not a Creature of your own providing?

Sir *Jeal.* She was of the Devil's providing for ought I know.

Patch. What have I done, Sir to merit your Displeasure?

Sir *Jeal.* I don't know which of you have done it; but you shall both suffer for it, till I can discover whose Guilt it is: Go get in there, I'll move you from this side of the House *(Pushes* Isabinda *in at the other Door, and locks it; puts the Key in his Pocket.)* I'll keep the Key my self: I'll try what Ghost will get into that Room. And now forsooth I'll wait on you down Stairs.

Patch. Ah, my poor Lady— Down Stairs, Sir, but I won't go out, Sir, till I have look'd up my Cloaths.

Sir *Jeal.* If thou wer't as naked as thou wer't born, thou should'st not stay to put on a Smock. Come along, I say, when your Mistress is marry'd you shall have your Rags, and every thing that belongs to you; but till then—

(Exit, pulling her out.

Patch. Oh! barbarous Usage for nothing.

Re-enter at the lower Door.

Sir *Jeal.* There, go, and, come no more within sight of my Habitation, these three Days, I charge you.

(Slaps the Door after her.

50*Patch.* Did ever any Body see such an old Monster!

Enter Charles.

Patch. Oh! Mr. *Charles* your Affairs and mine are in an ill Posture.

Char. I am immur'd to the Frowns of Fortune: But what has befal'n thee?

Patch. Sir *Jealous,* whose suspicious Nature's always on the Watch; nay, even whilst one Eye sleeps, the other keeps Sentinel: Upon sight of you, flew into such a violent Passion, that I cou'd find no Stratagem to appease him, but in spight of all Arguments, lock'd his Daughter into his own Apartment, and turn'd me out of Doors.

Char. Ha! oh, *Isabinda.*

Patch. And swears she shall neither see Sun nor Moon, till she is *Don Diego Babinetto*'s Wife, who arrived last Night, and is expected with impatience.

Char. He dies, yes, by all the Wrongs of Love he shall; here will I plant my self, and thro' my Breast he shall make his Passage, if he enters.

Patch. A most heroick Resolution. There might be ways found out more to your Advantage. Policy is often preferr'd to open force.

Char. I apprehend you not.

Patch. What think you of personating this *Spaniard,* imposing upon the Father, and marrying your Mistress by his own Consent.

Char. Say'st thou so my Angel! Oh cou'd that be done, my Life to come wou'd be too short to recompence thee: But how can I do that, when I neither know what Ship he came in, nor from what part of *Spain;* who recommends him, nor how attended.

Patch. I can solve all this. He is from *Madrid,* his Father's Name *Don Pedro Questo Portento Babinetto.* Here's a Letter of his to Sir *Jealous,* which he drop'd one Day; you understand *Spanish,* and the Hand may be counterfeited: You conceive me, Sir.

51**H2***Char.* My better Genius, thou hast reviv'd my drooping Soul: I'll about it instantly. Come to my Lodgings, and we'll concert Matters.

(Exeunt.

S C E N E a Garden Gate open, *Scentwell* waiting within.

Enter Sir George Airy.

Sir *Geo.* So, this is the Gate, and most invitingly open: If there shou'd be a Blunderbuss here now, what a dreadful Ditty wou'd my Fall make for Fools; and what a Jest for the Wits; how my Name wou'd be roar'd about Streets. Well I'll venture all.

Scentw. Hist, hist, Sir *George Airy*—

(Enters.

Sir *Geo.* A Female Voice, thus far I'm safe, my Dear.

Scentw. No, I'm not your Dear, but I'll conduct you to her, give me your Hand; you must go thro' many a dark Passage and dirty Step before you arrive—

Sir *Geo.* I know I must before I arrive at Paradise; therefore be quick my charming Guide.

Scentw. For ought you know; come, come your Hand and away.

Sir *Geo.* Here, here Child, you can't be half so swift as my Desires.

(Exeunt.

S C E N E the House.

27

Enter Miranda.

Miran. Well, let me reason a little with my mad self. Now don't I transgress all Rules to
venture upon a Man, without the Advice of the Grave and Wise; but then a rigid knavish
Guardian who wou'd have marry'd me. To whom? Even to his nauseous self, or no Body:
Sir *George* is what I have try'd in Conversation, inquir'd into his Character, am satisfied in both.
Then his Love; who wou'd have given a hundred Pound only to have seen a Woman he had not
infinitely loved? So I find my liking him has furnish'd me with Arguments enough of his side; and
now the only Doubt remains whether he will come or no.

52

Enter Scentwell.

Scentw. That's resolv'd, Madam, for here's the Knight.

Exit Scentwell.

Sir Geo. And do I once more behold that lovely Object, whose Idea fills my Mind, and
forms my pleasing Dreams!

Miran. What beginning again in Heroicks!— Sir *George*, don't you remember how little
Fruit your last Prodigal Oration produced, not one bare single Word in answer.

Sir Geo. Ha! the Voice of my *Incognita*— Why did you take Ten Thousand ways to captivate
a Heart your Eyes alone had vanquish'd?

Miran. Prithee, no more of these Flights; for our Time's but short, and we must fall into
Business: Do you think we can agree on that same terrible Bugbear, *Matrimony*, without heartily
Repenting on both sides.

Sir Geo. It has been my wish since first my longing Eyes beheld ye.

Miran. And your happy Ears drank in the pleasing News, I had Thirty Thousand Pound.

Sir Geo. Unkind! Did I not offer you in those purchas'd Minutes to run the Risque of your
Fortune, so you wou'd but secure that lovely Person to my Arms.

Miran. Well, if you have such Love and Tenderness, (since our Woing has been short) pray
reserve it for our future Days, to let the World see we are Lovers after Wedlock; 'twill be a
Novelty—

Sir Geo. Haste then, and let us tye the Knot, and prove the envy'd Pair—

Miran. Hold! not so fast, I have provided better than to venture on dangerous
Experiments headlong— My *Guardian*, trusting to my dissembled Love, has given up my Fortune
to my own dispose; but with this *Proviso*, that he to Morrow morning weds me. He is now gone
to *Doctors Commons* for a License.

Sir Geo. Ha, a License!

Miran. But I have planted Emissaries that infallibly take him down to *Epsom*, under
pretence that a Brother Usurer of 53his, is to make him his Executor; the thing on Earth he
covets.

Sir Geo. 'Tis his known Character.

Miran. Now my Instruments confirm him, this Man is dying, and he sends me word he
goes this Minute; it must be to Morrow e'er he can be undeceiv'd. That time is ours.

Sir Geo. Let us improve it then, and settle on our coming Years, endless, endless
Happiness.

Miran. I dare not stir till I hear he's on the Road—then I and my Writings, the most
material point, are soon removed.

Sir Geo. I have one Favour to ask, if it lies in your power, you wou'd be a Friend to
poor *Charles*, tho' the Son of this tenacious Man: He is as free from all his Vices, as Nature and a
good Education can make him; and what now I have vanity enough to hope will induce you, he is
the Man on Earth I love.

Miran. I never was his Enemy, and only put it on as it help'd my Designs on his Father. If
his Uncle's Estate ought to be in his Possession, which I shrewdly suspect, I may do him a
singular piece of Service.

Sir Geo. You are all Goodness.

Enter Scentwell.

Scentw. Oh, Madam, my Master and Mr. *Marplot* are just coming into the House.

Miran. Undone, undone! if he finds you here in this Crisis, all my Plots are unravell'd.

Sir Geo. What shall I do! can't I get back into the Garden?

Scentw. Oh, no! he comes up those Stairs.

Miran. Here, here, here! can you condescend to stand behind this Chimney-Board,
Sir *George?*

Sir Geo. Any where, any where, dear Madam, without Ceremony.

Scentw. Come, come, Sir; lie close—

(They put him behind the Chimney-Board.

28

Enter Sir Francis *and* Marplot: *Sir* Francis *peeling an Orange.*

Sir Fran. I cou'd not go, tho' 'tis upon Life and Death, without taking leave of dear *Chargee.* Besides, this Fellow buz'd in my Ears, that thou might'st be so desperate to shoot that wild Rake which haunts the Garden-Gate; and that wou'd bring us into Trouble, dear—

Miran. So, *Marplot* brought you back then: I am oblig'd to him for that, I'm sure—

(Frowning at Marplot *aside.*

Marpl. By her Looks she means she is not oblig'd to me. I have done some Mischief now, but what I can't imagine.

Sir Fran. Well, *Chargee,* I have had three Messengers to come to *Epsom* to my Neighbour *Squeezum's* who, for all his vast Riches, is departing.

(Sighs.

Marpl. Ay, see what all you Usurers must come to.

Sir Fran. Peace, ye young Knave! Some Forty Years hence I may think on't— But, *Chargee,* I'll be with thee to Morrow, before those pretty Eyes are open; I will, I will, *Chargee,* I'll rouze you, I saith.— Here Mrs. *Scentwell,* lift up your Lady's Chimney-Board, that I may throw my Peel in, and not litter her Chamber.

Miran. Oh my Stars! what will become of us now?

Scentw. Oh, pray Sir, give it me; I love it above all things in Nature, indeed I do.

Sir Fran. No, no, Hussy; you have the Green Pip already, I'll have no more Apothecary's Bills.

(Goes towards the Chimney.

Miran. Hold, hold, hold, dear *Gardee,* I have a, a, a, a Monkey shut up there; and if you open it before the Man comes that is to tame it, 'tis so wild 'twill break all my China, or get away, and that wou'd break my Heart; for I am fond on't to Distraction, next thee, dear *Gardee.*

(In a flattering Tone.

Sir Fran. Well, well, *Chargee,* I wont open it; she shall have her Monkey, poor Rogue; here throw this Peel out of the Window.

(Exit Scentwell.

Marpl. A Monkey, dear Madam, let me see it; I can tame 55 a Monkey as well as the best of them all. Oh how I love the little Minatures of Man.

Miran. Be quiet, Mischief, and stand farther from the Chimney— You shall not see my Monkey—why sure—

(Striving with him.

Marpl. For Heaven's sake, dear Madam, let me but peep, to see if it be as pretty as my Lady *Fiddle-Faddle's.* Has it got a Chain?

Miran. Not yet, but I design it one shall last its Life-time: Nay, you shall not see it— Look, *Gardee,* how he teazes me!

Sir Fran. (Getting between him and the Chimney.) Sirrah, Sirrah, let my *Chargee's* Monkey alone, or *Bambo* shall fly about your Ears. What is there no dealing with you?

Marpl. Pugh, pox of the Monkey! here's a Rout: I wish he may Rival you.

Enter a Servant.

Serv. Sir, they put two more Horses in the Coach, as you order'd, and 'tis ready at the Door.

Sir Fran. Well, I'm going to be Executor, better for thee, Jewel. B'ye *Chargee,* one Buss!— I'm glad thou hast got a a Monkey to divert thee a little.

Miran. Thank'e, dear *Gardee.*— Nay, I'll see you to the Coach.

Sir Fran. That's kind, adod.

Miran. Come along, Impertinence.

(To Marplot.

Marpl. (Stepping back.) Egad, I will see the Monkey: Now *(Lifts up the Board, and discovers Sir* George.*)* Oh Lord, Oh Lord! Thieves, Thieves, Murder!

Sir Geo. Dam'e, you unlucky Dog! 'tis I, which way shall I get out, shew me instantly, or I'll cut your Throat.

Marpl. Undone, undone! At that Door there. But hold, hold, break that China, and I'll bring you off.

(He runs off at the Corner, and throws down some China.
Re-enter Sir Francis, Miranda, *and* Scentwell.

Sir Fran. Mercy on me! what's the matter?

Miran. Oh, you Toad! what have you done?

56*Marpl.* No great harm, I beg of you to forgive me: Longing to see the Monkey, I did but just raise up the Board, and it flew over my Shoulders, scratch'd all my Face, broke yon' China, and whisk'd out of the Window.

Sir Fran. Was ever such an unlucky Rogue! Sirrah, I forbid you my House. Call the Servants to get the Monkey again; I wou'd stay my self to look it, but that you know my earnest Business.

Scentw. Oh my Lady will be the best to lure it back; all them Creatures love my Lady extremely.

Miran. Go, go, dear *Gardee*; I hope I shall recover it.

Sir Fran. B'ye, by'e, Dear'e. Ah, Mischief, how you look now! B'ye, b'ye.

(*Exit.*

Miran. *Scentwell*, see him in the Coach, and bring me word.

Scentw. Yes, Madam.

Miran. So, Sir, you have done your Friend a signal piece of Service, I suppose.

Marpl. Why look you, Madam! if I have committed a fault, thank your self; no Man is more Serviceable when I am let into a Secret, nor none more Unlucky at finding it out. Who cou'd divine your Meaning, when you talk'd of a Blunderbuss, who thought of a Rendevous? and when you talk'd of a Monkey, who the Devil dreamt of Sir *George*?

Miran. A sign you converse but little with our Sex, when you can't reconcile Contradictions.

Enter Scentwell.

Scentw. He's gone, Madam, as fast as the Coach, and Six can carry him.

Enter Sir George.

Sir Geo. Then I may appear.

Marpl. Dear, Sir *George*, make my Peace! On my Soul, I did not think of you.

Sir Geo. I dare swear thou didst not. Madam, I beg you to forgive him.

Miran. Well, Sir *George*, if he can be secret.

57I*Marpl.* Ods heart, Madam, I'm as secret as a Priest when I'm trusted.

Sir Geo. Why 'tis with a Priest our Business is at present.

Scentw. Madam, here's Mrs. *Isabinda*'s Woman to wait on you.

Miran. Bring her up.

Enter Patch.

How do'e, Mrs. *Patch*, what News from your Lady?

Patch. That's for your private Ear, Madam. Sir *George*, there's a Friend of yours has an urgent Occasion for your Assistance.

Sir Geo. His Name.

Patch. *Charles*.

Marpl. Ha! then there is something a-foot that I know nothing of. I'll wait on you, Sir *George*.

Sir Geo. A third Person may not be proper perhaps; as soon as I have dispatch'd my own Affairs, I am at his Service. I'll send my Servant to tell him, I'll wait upon him in half an Hour.

Miran. How come you employ'd in this Message, Mrs. *Patch*?

Patch. Want of Business, Madam. I am discharg'd by my Master, but hope to serve my Lady still.

Miran. How discharg'd! you must tell me the whole Story within.

Patch. With all my Heart, Madam.

Marpl. Pish! Pox, I wish I were fairly out of the House. I find Marriage is the end of this Secret: And now I am half mad to know what *Charles* wants him for.

(*Aside.*

Sir Geo. Madam, I'm doubly press'd, by Love and Friendship: This Exigence admits of no delay. Shall we make *Marplot* of the Party?

Miran. If you'll run the Hazard, Sir *George*; I believe he means well.

Marpl. Nay, nay, for my part, I desire to be let into nothing: I'll begon, therefore pray don't mistrust me.

(*Going.*

Sir Geo. So now has he a mind to be gone to *Charles*: but not knowing what Affairs he may have upon his Hands at 58present, I'm resolv'd he sha'n't stir: No, Mr. *Marplot*, you must not leave us, we want a third Person.

(*Takes hold of him.*

Marpl. I never had more mind to be gone in my Life.

Miran. Come along then; if we fail in the Voyage, thank your self for taking this ill starr'd Gentleman on Board.

Sir Geo.

That Vessel ne'er can Unsuccessful prove,
Whose Freight is Beauty, and whose Pilot Love.

The End of the Fourth ACT.

ACT the Fifth.

Enter Miranda, Patch, *and* Scentwell.

Miran.

WELL, *Patch,* I have done a strange bold thing! my Fate is determin'd, and Expectation is no more. Now to avoid the Impertinence and Roguery of an old Man, I have thrown my self into the Extravagance of a young one; if he shou'd despise, slight or use me ill, there's no Remedy from a Husband, but the Grave; and that's a terrible Sanctuary to one of my Age and Constitution.

Patch. O fear not, Madam, you'll find your account in Sir *George Airy;* it is impossible a Man of Sense shou'd use a Woman ill, indued with Beauty, Wit and Fortune. It must be the Lady's fault, if she does not wear the unfashionable Name of Wife easie, when nothing but Complaisance and good Humour is requisite on either side to make them happy.

Miran. I long till I am out of this House, lest any Accident shou'd bring my *Guardian* back. *Scentwell,* put my best Jewels into the little Casket, slip them, into thy Pocket, and let us march off to Sir.*Jealous's.*

Scentw. It shall be done, Madam.

(Exit Scentwell.

59**I2***Patch.* Sir *George* will be impatient, Madam; if their Plot succeeds, we shall be well receiv'd; if not, he will be able to protect us. Besides, I long to know how my young Lady fares.

Miran. Farewell, old *Mammon,* and thy detested Walls; 'twill be no more sweet Sir *Francis,* I shall be compell'd to the odious Task of Dissembling no longer to get my own, and coax him with the wheedling Names of my *Precious,* my *Dear,* dear *Gardee.* Oh Heavens!

Enter Sir Francis *behind.*

Sir Fran. Ah, my sweet *Chargee,* don't be frighted. *(She starts.)*But thy poor *Gardee* has been abused, cheated, fool'd, betray'd, but no Body knows by whom.

Miran. (Aside.) Undone! past Redemption.

Sir Fran. What won't you speak to me, *Chargee!*

Miran. I'm so surpriz'd with Joy to see you, I know not what to say.

Sir Fran. Poor, dear Girl! But do'e know that my Son, or some such Rogue, to rob or murder me, or both, contriv'd this Journey? For upon the Road I met my Neighbour *Squeezum* well, and coming to Town.

Miran. Good lack, good lack! what Tricks are there in this World!

Enter Scentwell, *with a Diamond Necklace in her Hand; not seeing Sir* Francis.

Scentw. Madam, be pleas'd to tye this Neck-lace on; for I can't get it into the—

(Seeing Sir Francis.

Miran. The Wench is a Fool, I think! cou'd you not have carry'd it to be mended, without putting it in the Box?

Sir Fran. What's the matter?

Miran. Only Dear'e, I bid her, I bid her— Your ill Usage has put every thing out of my Head. But won't you go, *Gardee,* and find out these Fellows, and have them punish'd! and, and—

Sir Fran. Where shou'd I look them, Child? No I'll sit me down contented with my Safety, nor stir out of my own Doors, till I go with thee to a Parson.

60*Miran. (Aside.)* If he goes into his Closet I am ruin'd. Oh! bless me in this Fright, I had forgot Mrs. *Patch.*

Patch. Ay, Madam, and I stay for your speedy Answer.

Miran. (Aside.) I must get him out of the House. Now assist me Fortune.

Sir Fran. Mrs. *Patch,* I profess I did not see you, how dost thou do, Mrs. *Patch;* well don't you repent leaving my *Chargee?*

Patch. Yes, every body must love her—but I came now— Madam, what did I come for, my Invention is at the last Ebb.

(Aside to Miranda.

Sir Fran. Nay, never Whisper, tell me.

Miran. She came, dear *Gardee* to invite me to her Lady's Wedding, and you shall go with me *Gardee,* 'tis to be done this Moment to a *Spanish* Merchant; Old Sir *Jealous* keeps on his Humour, the first Minute he sees her, the next he marries her.

Sir Fran. Ha, ha, ha, I'd go if I thought the sight of Matrimony wou'd tempt *Chargee* to perform her Promise: There was a smile, there was a consenting Look with those pretty Twinklers, worth a Million. Ods precious, I am happier than the Great *Mogul,* the Emperour

31

of *China*, or all the Potentates that are not in Wars. Speak, confirm it, make me leap out of my Skin.

Miran. When one has resolv'd, 'tis in vain to stand shall I, shall I, if ever I marry, positively this is my Wedding Day.

Sir Fran. Oh! happy, happy Man— Verily I will beget a Son, the first Night shall disinherit that Dog, *Charles.* I have Estate enough to purchase a Barony, and be the immortalizing the whole Family of the Gripes.

Miran. Come then *Gardee,* give me thy Hand, let's to this House of *Hymen.*
My Choice is fix'd, let good or ill betide,
Sir Fran.
The joyful Bridegroom, I
Miran.
And I the happy Bride.

(*Exeunt.*

61

Enter Sir Jealous *meeting a Servant.*

Serv. Sir, here's a couple of Gentlemen enquire for you; one of 'em calls himself *Seignor Diego Babinetto.*

Sir Jeal. Ha! *Seignor Babinetto!* Admit 'em instantly— Joyful Minute; I'll have my Daughter marry'd to Night.

Enter Charles *in* Spanish *Habit, with Sir* George *drest like a Merchant.*

Sir Jeal. *Senior, beso Las Manos vuestra merced es muy bien venido en esta tierra.*

Char. Senhor, soy muy humilde, y muy obligado Cryado de vuestra merced: Mi Padre Embia a vuestra merced, los mas profondos de sus respetos; y a Commissionado este Mercadel Ingles, de concluyr un negocio, que me Haze el mas dichoso hombre del mundo, Haziendo me su yerno.

Sir Jeal. I am glad on't, for I find I have lost much of my *Spanish.* Sir, I am your most humble Servant. *Seignor Don Diego Babinetto* has inform'd me that you are Commission'd by *Seignor Don Pedro,* &c. his worthy Father.

Sir Geo. To see an Affair of Marriage Consummated between a Daughter of yours, and *Seignor Diego Babinetto* his Son here. True, Sir, such a Trust is repos'd in me as that Letter will inform you. I hope 'twill pass upon him. *(Aside.)*

(*Gives him a Letter.*

Sir Jeal. Ay, 'tis his Hand.

(*Seems to read.*

Sir Geo. Good —— you have counterfeited to a Nicety, *Charles.*

(*Aside to* Charles.

Char. If the whole Plot succeeds as well, I'm happy.

Sir Jeal. Sir I find by this, that you are a Man of Honour and Probity; I think, Sir, he calls you *Meanwell.*

Sir Geo. Meanwell is my Name, Sir.

Sir Jeal. A very good Name, and very Significant.

Char. Yes, Faith if he knew all.

(*Aside.*

Sir Jeal. For to Mean-well is to be honest, and to be honest is the Virtue of a Friend, and a Friend is the Delight and Support of Human Society.

Sir Geo. You shall find that I'll Discharge the part of a Friend in what I have undertaken, Sir *Jealous.*

62*Char.* But little does he think to whom.

(*Aside.*

Sir Geo. Therefore, Sir, I must intreat the Presence of your fair Daughter, and the Assistance of your Chaplain; for *Seignor Don Pedro* strictly enjoyn'd me to see the Marriage Rites perform'd as soon as we should arrive, to avoid the Accidental Overtures of *Venus.*

Sir Jeal. Overtures of *Venus!*

Sir Geo. Ay, Sir, that is, those little Hawking Females that traverse the Park, and the Play-house to put off their damag'd Ware—they fasten upon Foreigners like Leeches, and watch their Arrival as carefully, as the *Kentish* Men do a Ship-wreck. I warrant you they have heard of him already.

Sir Jeal. Nay, I know this Town swarms with them.

Sir Geo. Ay, and then you know the *Spaniards* are naturally Amorous, but very Constant, the first Face fixes 'em, and it may be dangerous to let him ramble e'er he is tied.

Char. Well hinted.

(*Aside.*

32

Sir *Jeal.* Pat to my Purpose— Well, Sir, there is but one thing more, and they shall be married instantly.

Char. Pray Heaven, that one thing more don't spoil all.

(Aside.

Sir *Jeal. Don Pedro* writ me Word in his last but one, that he design'd the Sum of Five Thousand Crowns by way of Joynture for my Daughter; and that it shou'd be paid into my Hand upon the Day of Marriage.

Char. Oh! the Devil.

(Aside.

Sir *Jeal.* In order to lodge it in some of our Funds, in case she should become a Widow, and return for *England.*

Sir *Geo.* Pox on't, this is an unlucky Turn. What shall I say?

(Aside.

Sir *Jeal.* And he does not mention one Word of it in this Letter.

Char. I don't know how he should.

(Aside.

Sir *Geo.* Humph! True, Sir *Jealous,* he told me such a Thing, but, but, but, but—he, he, he, he—he did not imagine that you would insist upon the very Day, for, for, for, for Money you know is dangerous returning by Sea, an, an, an, an—

63Char. Zounds, say we have brought it in Commodities.

(Aside to Sir George.

Sir *Geo.* And so Sir, he has sent it in Merchandize, *Tobacco, Sugars, Spices, Limons,* and so forth, which shall be turn'd into Money with all Expedition: In the mean time, Sir, if you please to accept of my Bond for Performance.

Sir *Jeal.* It is enough, Sir, I am so pleas'd with the Countenance of *Seignor Diego,* and the Harmony of your Name, that I'll take your Word, and will fetch my Daughter this Moment. Within there *(Enter Servant)* desire Mr. *Tackum* my Neighbour's Chaplain to walk hither.

Serv. Yes, Sir.

(Exit.

Sir *Jeal.* Gentlemen, I'll return in an Instant.

(Exit.

Char. Wondrous well. Let me embrace thee.

Sir *Geo.* Egad that 5000 *l.* had like to have ruin'd the Plot.

Char. But that's over! And if Fortune throws no more Rubs in our way.

Sir *Geo.* Thou'lt carry the Prize—but hist, here he comes.

Enter Sir Jealous, *dragging in* Isabinda.

Sir *Jeal.* Come along, you stubborn Baggage you, come along.

Isab.

Oh hear me, Sir! hear me but speak one Word,
Do not destroy my everlasting Peace;
My Soul abhors this Spaniard you have chose
Nor can I wed him without being curst.

Sir *Jeal.* How's that!

Isab.

Let this Posture move your tender Nature. (Kneels.
For ever will I hang upon these Knees;
Nor loose my Hands till you cut off my hold,
If you refuse to hear me, Sir.

Char. Oh! that I cou'd discover my self to her.

(Aside.

Sir *Geo.* Have a care what you do. You had better trust to his Obstinacy.

(Aside.

Sir *Jeal.* Did you ever see such a perverse Slut: Off I say Mr.*Meanwell* pray help me a little.

64Sir *Geo.* Rise, Madam, and do not disoblige your Father, who has provided a Husband worthy of you, one that will Love you equal with his Soul, and one that you will Love, when once you know him.

Isab. Oh! never, never. Cou'd I suspect that Falshood in my Heart, I wou'd this Moment tear it from my Breast, and streight present him with the Treacherous Part.

Char. Oh! my charming faithful Dear.

(Aside.

Sir *Jeal.* Falshood! why, who the Devil are you in Love with? Ha! Don't provoke me, for by St. *Jago* I shall beat you, Housewife.

33

Char. Heaven forbid; for I shall infallibly discover my self if he should.

(Aside.

Sir *Geo.* Have Patience, Madam! and look at him: Why will you prepossess your self against a Man that is Master of all the Charms you would desire in a Husband?

Sir *Jeal.* Ay, look at him, *Isabinda, Senior pase vind adelante.*

Char. My Heart bleeds to see her grieve, whom I imagin'd would with Joy receive me. *Seniora obligue me vuestra merced de sumano.*

Sir *Jeal. (Pulling up her Head.)* Hold up your Head, hold up your Head, Housewife, and look at him: Is there a properer, handsomer, better shap'd Fellow in *England,* ye Jade you. Ha! see, see the obstinate Baggage shuts her Eyes; by St. *Jago,* I have a good Mind to beat 'em out.

(Pushes her down.

Isab.
Do then, Sir, kill me, kill me instantly.
'Tis much the kinder Action of the Two,
For 'twill be worse than Death to wed him.

Sir *Geo.* Sir *Jealous,* you are too passionate. Give me leave, I'll try by gentle Words to work her to your Purpose.

Sir *Jeal.* I pray do, Mr. *Meanwell,* I pray do; she'll break my Heart.*(weeps)* There is in that, Jewels of the Value of 3000 *l.* which were her Mother's; and a Paper wherein I have settled one half of my Estate upon her now, and the whole when I dye. But provided she marries this Gentleman, else by St. *Jago,* I'll turn her out of Doors to beg or starve. Tell her this, Mr. *Meanwell,* pray do.

(Walks off.

65**K**Sir *Geo.* Ha! this is beyond Expectation— Trust to me, Sir, I'll lay the dangerous Consequence of disobeying you at this Juncture before her, I warrant you.

Char. A sudden Joy runs thro' my Heart like a propitious Omen.

(Aside.

Sir *Geo.* Come, Madam, do not blindly cast your Life away just in the Moment you would wish to have it.

Isab. Pray cease your Trouble, Sir, I have no Wish but sudden Death to free me from this hated *Spaniard.* If you are his Friend inform him what I say; my Heart is given to another Youth, whom I love with the same strength of Passion that I hate this *Diego;* with whom, if I am forc'd to wed, my own Hand shall cut the Gordian Knot.

Sir *Geo.* Suppose this *Spaniard* which you strive to shun should be the very Man to whom you'd flye?

Isab. Ha!

Sir *Geo.* Would you not blame your rash Result, and curse those Eyes that would not look on *Charles.*

Isab. On *Charles!* Oh you have inspir'd new Life, and collected every wandring Sense. Where is he? Oh! let me flye into his Arms.

(Rises.

Sir *Geo.* Hold, hold, hold, 'Zdeath, Madam, you'll ruin all, your Father believes him to be *Seignor Barbinetto.* Compose your self a little, pray Madam.

(He runs to Sir Jealous.

Char. Her Eyes declare she knows me.

(Aside.

Sir *Geo.* She begins to hear Reason, Sir, the fear of being turn'd out of Doors has done it.

(Runs back to Isabinda.

Isab. 'Tis he, oh! my ravish'd Soul.

Sir *Geo.* Take heed, Madam, you don't betray your self. Seem with Reluctance to consent, or you are undone, *(runs to Sir Jealous,)*speak gently to her, Sir, I'm sure she'll yield, I see it in her Face.

Sir *Jeal.* Well, *Isabinda,* can you refuse to bless a Father, whose only Care is to make you happy, as Mr. *Meanwell* has inform'd you. Come, wipe thy Eyes; nay, prithee do, or thou wilt break thy Father's Heart; see thou bring'st the 66Tears in mine to think of thy undutiful Carriage to me.

(Weeps.

Isab. Oh! do not weep, Sir, your Tears are like a Ponyard to my Soul; do with me what you please, I am all Obedience.

Sir *Jeal.* Ha! then thou art my Child agen.

Sir *Geo.* 'Tis done, and now Friend the Day's thy own.

Char. The happiest of my Life, if nothing Intervene.

Sir Jeal. And wilt thou love him?

Isab. I will endeavour it, Sir.

Enter Servant.

Serv. Sir, Here is Mr. *Tackum.*

Sir Jeal. Show him into the Parlour—*Senior tome vind sueipora; cete Momenta les Junta les Manos.*

(Gives her to Charles.

Char. Oh! transport—*Senior yo la recibo Como se deve un Tesoro tan Grande.* Oh! my Joy, my Life, my Soul.

(Embrace.

Isab. My Faithful everlasting Comfort.

Sir Jeal. Now, Mr. *Meanwell* let's to the Parson,
Who, by his Art will join this Pair for Life,
Make me the happiest Father, her the happiest Wife.

(Exit.

S C E N E Changes to the Street before Sir *Jealous*'s Door.

Enter Marplot, *Solus.*

Marpl. I have hunted all over the Town for *Charles*, but can't find him; and by *Whisper*'s scouting at the End of the Street, I suspect he must be in this House again. I'm inform'd too that he has borrow'd a *Spanish* Habit out of the *Play-house.* What can it mean?

67**K2**

Enter a Servant of Sir Jealous*'s to him, out of the House.*

Hark'e, Sir, do you belong to this House?

Serv. Yes, Sir.

Marpl. Pray can you tell if there be a Gentleman in it in *Spanish* Habit?

Serv. There is a *Spanish* Gentleman within, that is just a going to marry my young Lady, Sir.

Marpl. Are you sure he is a *Spanish* Gentleman?

Serv. I'm sure he speaks no *English*, that I hear of.

Marpl. Then that can't be him I want; for 'tis an *English* Gentleman, tho' I suppose he may be dress'd like a *Spaniard*, that I enquire after.

Serv. Ha! who knows but this may be an Impostor? I'll inform my Master; for if he shou'd be impos'd upon, he'll beat us all round. *(Aside.)* Pray, come in, Sir, and see if this be the Person you enquire for.

S C E N E Changes to the Inside the House.

Enter Marplot.

Marpl. So, this was a good Contrivance: If this be *Charles*, now will he wonder how I found him out.

Enter Servant and Jealous.

Sir Jeal. What is your earnest Business, Blockhead, that you must speak with me before the Ceremony's past? Ha! who's this?

Serv. Why this Gentleman, Sir, wants another Gentleman in. *Spanish* Habit, he says.

Sir Jeal. In *Spanish* Habit! 'tis some Friend of Seignior *Don Diego*'s, I warrant. Sir, I suppose you wou'd speak with Seignior *Barbinetto*—

Marpl. Hy-day! what the Devil does he say now!— Sir, I don't understand you.

68*Sir Jeal.* Don't you understand *Spanish*, Sir?

Marpl. Not I indeed, Sir.

Sir Jeal. I thought you had known Seignior *Barbinetto.*

Marpl. Not I, upon my word, Sir.

Sir Jeal. What then you'd speak with his Friend, the *English* Merchant, Mr. *Meanwell.*

Marpl. Neither, Sir; not I.

Sir Jeal. Why who are you then, Sir? and what do you want?

(In an angry Tone.

Marpl. Nay, nothing at all, not I, Sir. Pox on him! I wish I were out, he begins to exalt his Voice, I shall be beaten agen.

Sir Jeal. Nothing at all, Sir! Why then what Business have you in my House? ha?

Serv. You said you wanted a Gentleman in *Spanish* Habit.

Marpl. Why ay, but his Name is neither *Barbinetto* nor *Meanwell.*

Sir Jeal. What is his Name then, Sirrah, ha? Now I look at you agen, I believe you are the Rogue threaten'd me with half a Dozen *Mirmidons*— Speak, Sir, who is it you look for? or, or—

Marpl. A terrible old Dog!— Why, Sir, only an honest young Fellow of my Acquaintance— I thought that here might be a Ball, and that he might have been here in a Masquerade; 'tis *Charles*, Sir *Francis Gripe*'s Son, because I know he us'd to come hither sometimes.

35

Sir *Jeal.* Did he so?— Not that I know of, I'm sure. Pray Heaven that this be Don *Diego*— If I shou'd be trick'd now— Ha! my Heart misgives me plaguily—within there! stop the Marriage— Run, Sirrah, call all my Servants! I'll be satisfy'd that this is Seignior*Pedro*'s Son e're he has my Daughter.

Marpl. Ha, Sir *George*, what have I done now ?

Enter Sir George *with a drawn Sword between the Scenes.*

Sir *Geo.* Ha! *Marplot*, here— Oh the unlucky Dog—what's the matter, Sir *Jealous?*

69Sir *Jeal.* Nay, I don't know the matter, Mr.*Meanwell.*

Marpl. Upon my Soul, Sir *George*—

(Going up to Sir Geo.

Sir *Jeal.* Nay then, I'm betray'd, ruin'd, undone: Thieves, Traytors, Rogues! *(Offers to go in.)* Stop the Marriage, I say—

Sir *Geo.* I say, go on Mr.*Tackum*— Nay, no Ent'ring here, I guard this Passage, old Gentleman; the Act and Deed were both your own, and I'll see 'em sign'd, or die for't.

Enter Servants.

Sir *Jeal.* A pox on the Act and Deed!— Fall on, knock him down.

Sir *Geo.* Ay, come on, Scoundrils! I'll prick your Jackets for you.

Sir *Jeal.* Z'ounds, Sirrah, I'll be Reveng'd on you.

(Beats Marplot.

Sir *Geo.* Ay, there your Vengeance is due; Ha, ha.

Marpl. Why, what do you beat me for? I ha'nt marry'd your Daughter.

Sir *Jeal.* Rascals! why don't you knock him down?

Serv. We are afraid of his Sword, Sir; if you'll take that from him, we'll knock him down presently.

Enter Charles *and* Isabinda.

Sir *Jeal.* Seize her then.

Char. Rascals, retire; she's my Wife, touch her if you dare, I'll make Dogs meat of you.

Sir *Jeal.* Ah! downright *English:*— Oh, oh, oh, oh!

Enter Sir Francis Gripe, Mirand, Patch, Scentwell, *and* Whisper.

Sir *Fran.* Into the House of Joy we Enter without knocking: Ha! I think 'tis the House of Sorrow, Sir *Jealous.*

Sir *Jeal.* Oh Sir *Francis!* are you come? What was this your Contrivance, to abuse, trick, and chouse me of my Child!

Sir *Fran.* My Contrivance! what do you mean?

Sir *Jeal.* No, you don't know your Son there in *Spanish* Habit.

70Sir *Fran.* How! my Son in *Spanish* Habit. Sirrah, you'll come to be hang'd; get out of my sight, ye Dog! get out of my sight.

Sir *Jeal.* Get out of your sight, Sir! Get out with your Bags; let's see what you'll give him now to maintain my Daughter on.

Sir *Fran.* Give him! He shall be never the better for a Penny of mine—and you might have look'd after your Daughter better, Sir*Jealous.* Trick'd, quotha! Egad, I think you design'd to trick me: But look ye, Gentlemen, I believe I shall trick you both. This Lady is my Wife, do you see? And my Estate shall descend only to the Heirs of her Body.

Sir *Geo.* Lawfully begotten by me— I shall be extremely oblig'd to you, Sir *Francis.*

Sir *Fran.* Ha, ha, ha, ha, poor Sir *George!* You see your Project was of no use. Does not your Hundred Pound stick in your Stomach? Ha, ha, ha.

Sir *Geo.* No faith, Sir *Francis*, this Lady has given me a Cordial for that.

(Takes her by the Hand.

Sir *Fran.* Hold, Sir, you have nothing to say to this Lady.

Sir *Geo.* Nor you nothing to do with my Wife, Sir.

Sir *Fran.* Wife, Sir!

Miran. Ay really, *Guardian*, 'tis even so. I hope you'll forgive my first Offence.

Sir *Fran.* What have you chous'd me out of my Consent, and your Writings then, Mistress, ha?

Miran. Out of nothing but my own, *Guardian.*

Sir *Jeal.* Ha, ha, ha, 'tis some Comfort at least to see you are over-reach'd as well as my self. Will you settle your Estate upon your Son now?

Sir *Fran.* He shall starve first.

Miran. That I have taken care to prevent. There, Sir, is the Writings of your Uncle's *Estate*, which has been your due these three Years.

(Gives Char. *Papers.*

Char. I shall study to deserve this Favour.

36

Sir Fran. What have you robb'd me too, Mistress! Egad I'll make you restore 'em.—— Huswife, I will so.

71*Sir Jeal.* Take care I don't make you pay the Arrears, Sir. 'Tis well it's no worse, since 'tis no better. Come, young Man, seeing thou hast out-witted me, take her, and Bless you both.

Char. I hope, Sir, you'll bestow your Blessing too, 'tis all I'll ask.

(Kneels.

Sir Fran. Confound you all!

(Exit.

Marpl. Mercy upon us! how he looks!

Sir Geo. Ha, ha, ne'er mind his Curses, *Charles,* thou'lt thrive not one jot the worse for 'em. Since this Gentleman is reconcil'd, we are all made happy.

Sir Jeal. I always lov'd Precaution, and took care to avoid Dangers. But when a thing was past, I ever had Philosophy to be easie.

Char. Which is the true sign of a great Soul: I lov'd your Daughter, and she me, and you shall have no reason to repent her Choice.

Isab. You will not blame me, Sir, for loving my own Country best.

Marpl. So here's every Body happy, I find, but poor *Pilgarlick.* I wonder what Satisfaction I shall have, for being cuff'd, kick'd, and beaten in your Service.

Sir Jeal. I have been a little too familiar with you, as things are fallen out; but since there's no help for't, you must forgive me.

Marpl. Egad I think so—— But provided that you be not so familiar for the future.

Sir Geo. Thou hast been an unlucky Rogue.

Marpl. But very honest.

Char. That I'll vouch for; and freely forgive thee.

Sir Geo. And I'll do you one piece of Service more, *Marplot,* I'll take care that Sir *Francis* make you Master of your Estate.

Marpl. That will make me as happy as any of you.

Patch. Your humble Servant begs leave to remind you, Madam.

Isab. Sir, I hope you'll give me leave to take *Patch* into favour again.

72*Sir Jeal.* Nay, let your Husband look to that, I have done with my Care.

Char. Her own Liberty shall always oblige me. Here's no Body but honest *Whisper* and Mrs. *Scentwell* to be provided for now. It shall be left to their Choice to Marry, or keep their Services.

Whisp. Nay then, I'll stick to my Master.

Scentw. Coxcomb! and I prefer my Lady before a Footman.

Sir Jeal. Hark, I hear Musick, the Fidlers smell a Wedding. What say you, young Fellows, will ye have a Dance?

Sir Geo. With all my Heart; call'em in.

A   D A N C E .

Sir Jeal. Now let us in and refresh our selves with a chearful Glass, in which we'll bury all Animosities: And

By my Example let all Parents move,
And never strive to cross their Childrens Love;
But still submit that Care to Providence above.

F I N I S

CPSIA information can be obtained
at www.ICGtesting.com
Printed in the USA
LVHW080413261122
733961LV00009BA/802